EARTHWORK OUT OF TUSCANY

Perugino.

EARTHWORK OUT OF TUSCANY >< BEING IMPRESSIONS AND TRANSLATIONS OF MAURICE HEWLETT WITH ILLUSTRATIONS BY JAMES KERR LAWSON >< ><

"*For as it is hurtful to drink wine or water alone; and as wine mingled with water is pleasant and delighteth the taste: even so speech, finely framed, delighteth the ears of them that read the story.*"— 2 MACCABEES XV. 39.

*New edition
With additional
Illustrations in
Photogravure*

New York
CHARLES SCRIBNER'S SONS
1911

To

MY FATHER

THIS LITTLE BOOK,

NOT AS BEING WORTHY, BUT AS ALL I HAVE,

IS DEDICATED

———

I cannot add one tendril to your bays,
Worn quietly where who love you sing your praise,
But I may stand
Among the household throng with lifted hand,
Upholding for sweet honour of the land
Your crown of days.

PREFACE TO THE SECOND EDITION

MY CRITICS—to whom, kind or unkind, I confess obligations—and the Public between them have produced, it appears, some sort of demand for this Second Edition. While I do not think it either polite or politic to enquire too deeply into reasons, I am not the man to disoblige them. It is sufficient for me that in a world indifferent well-peopled five hundred souls have bought or acquired my book, and that other hundreds have signified their desire to do likewise. Nevertheless—the vanity of authors being notoriously hard-rooted—I must own to my mortification in the discovery that not more than two in every hundred who have read me have known what I was at. I have been told it is a good average, but, with defer-ence, I don't think so. No man has any right to take beautiful and simple things

out of their places, wrap them up in a tissue
of his own conceits, and hand them about
the universe for gods and men to wonder
upon. If he must convey simple things let
him convey them simply. If I, for instance,
must steal a loaf of bread, would it not be
better to walk out of the shop with it under
my coat than to call for it in a hansom
and hoodwink the baker with a forged
cheque on Coutts's bank ? Surely. If, then,
I go to Italy, and convey the hawthorn-
scent of Della Robbia, the straining of
Botticelli to express the ineffable, the mellow
autumn tones of the life of Florence ; if I
do this, and make a parade of my magnani-
mity in permitting the household to divide
the spoil, how on earth should I mar all my
bravery by giving people what they don't
want, or turn double knave by fobbing them
off with an empty box ?

I had hoped to have done better than this.
I tried to express in the title of my book
what I thought I had done ; more, I was
bold enough to assume that, having weath-

*ered the title, my readers would find a
smooth channel with leading-lights enough
to bring them sound to port.* Mea culpa !
*I believe I was wrong. The book has been
read as a collection of essays and stories
and dialogues only pulled together by the
binder's tapes; as otherwise disjointed, frag-
mentary,* décousue, *a "piebald monstrous
book," a sort of* kous-kous, *made out
of the odds and ends of a scribbler's
note-book. Some have liked some morsels,
others other morsels : it has been a matter
of the luck of the fork. Very few, one only
to my knowledge, can have seen the thing as
it presented itself to my flattering eye—not
as a pudding, not as a case of confectionery
even, but as a little sanctuary of images such
as a pious heathen might make of his earthenware gods. Let us be serious : listen.
The thing is Criticism ; but some of it is
criticism by trope and figure. I hope that
is plain enough.*

*When the first man heard his first thun-
derstorm he said (or Human Nature has*

bettered itself), " *Certainly a God is angry.*" *When after a night of doubt and heaviness the sun rose out of the sea, the sea kindled, and all its waves laughed innumerably, again he said, " God is stirring. Joy cometh in the morning.*" *Even in saying so much he was making images, poor man, for one's soul is as dumb as a fish and can only talk by signs. But by degrees, as his hand grew obedient to his heart, he set to work to make more lasting images of these gods—Thunder Gods, Gods of the Sun and the Morning. And as these gods were the sum of the best feelings he had, so the images of them were the best things he made. And that goes on now whenever a young man sees something new or strange or beautiful. He wonders, he falls on his face, he would say his prayers; he rises up, he would sing a pæan. But he is dumb, the wretch! He must make images. This he does because Necessity drives him : this I have done. And part of the world calls the result Criticism, and another*

*part says, It may be Art.   But I know that
it is the struggling of a dumb man to find
an outlet, and I call it Religion.*

*" God first made man, and straightway man made
      God :
No wonder if a tang of that same sod,
Whereout we issued at a breath, should cling
To all we fashion.   We can only plod
Lit by a starveling candle ; and we sing
Of what we can remember of the road."*

*The vague informed, the lovely indefinite
defined : that is Art.   As a sort of* pâte
sur pâte *comes Criticism, to do for Art
what Art does for life.   I have tried in this
book to be the artist at second-hand, to
make pictures of pictures, images of images,
poems of poems.   You may call it Criticism,
you may call it Art : I call it Religion.   It
is making the best thing I can out of the best
things I feel.*

*One thing is very plain ; whatever may
be said of my pictures, Mr. Kerr Lawson in
his has brought the very breath of the places*

he, you, and I love. I come jigging with my commentary at his heels, and am well content; for I know I shall have a chance of a hearing while he holds your eyes.

LONDON, 1898.

ADVERTISEMENT

POLITE reader, you who have travelled
Italy, *it will not be unknown to you that
the humbler sort in that country have ever
believed certain spots and recesses of their
land — as wells, mountain-paths, farm-
steads, groves of ilex or olive, quiet pine-
woods, creeks or bays of the sea, and such
like hidden ways—to be the chosen resort of
familiar spirits, baleful or beneficent, fate-
ridden or amenable to prayer, half divine,
wholly out of rule or ordering; which rustic
deities and* genii locorum, *if it was not
needful to propitiate, it was fascination to
observe. It is believed of them in the hill-
country round about* Perugia *and in the
quieter parts of* Tuscany, *that they are still
present, tolerated of God by reason of their
origin (which is, indeed, that of the very
soil whose effluence they are), chastened,
circumscribed, and, as it were, combed or*

pared of evil desire and import. To them or their avatars (it matters little which) the rude people still bow down; they still humour them with gifts of flowers, songs, or artless customs (as of May-day or the Giorno de' Grilli); you may still see wayside shrines, votive tablets, humble offerings, set in a farm-wall or country hedge, starry and fresh as a patch of yellow flowers in a rye-field. If you say that they have made gods in their own image, you do not convince them of Sin, for they do as their betters. If you say their gods are earthy, they reply by asking, "What then are we?" For they will admit, and you cannot deny, earthiness to have at least a part in all of us. And you are forbidden to call this unhappy, since God made all. Out of the drenched earth whence these worshippers arose, they made their rough-cast gods; out of the same earth they still mould images to speak the presentment of them which they have. Out of that earth, I, a northern image-maker, have set up my conceits of *their informing spirits, of the spirits of themselves, their soil, and the fair works they have accomplished.* So I have called *this book* Earthwork out of Tuscany. Qui habet aures ad audiendum audiat.

LONDON, 1895.

CONTENTS

ILLUSTRATIONS IN
PHOTOGRAVURE

xvii

ILLUSTRATIONS OTHER THAN PHOTOGRAVURE

PROEM

A LTHOUGH you know your Italy well,
you ask me, who see her now for
the first time, to tell you how I find her;
how she sinks into me; wherein she fulfils,
and wherein fails to fulfil, certain dreams
and fancies of mine (old amusements of
yours) about her. Here, truly, you show
yourself the diligent collector of human
documents, your friends have always believed you; for I think it can only be appetite for acquisition, to see how a man
recognisant of the claims of modernity in
Art bears the first brunt of the Old Masters'
assault, that tempts you to risk a *réchauffée*
of Paul Bourget and Walter Pater, with
ana lightly culled from Symonds, and, perchance, the questionable support of ponder-
ous references out of Burckhardt. In spite
of my waiver of the title, you relish the
notion of a Modern face to face with Botticelli and Mantegna and Perugino (to say

nothing of that Giotto who had so much to say !), artists in whom, you think and I agree, certain impressions strangely positive of many vanished aspects of life remain to be accounted for, and (it may be) reconciled with modern visions of Art and Beauty. Well ! I am flattered and touched by such confidence in my powers of expression and your own of endurance. I look upon you as a late-in-time Mæcenas, generously re-solved to defray the uttermost charge of weariness, that a young writer may be en-couraged to unfold himself and splash in the pellucid Tuscan air. I cannot assert that you are performing an act of charity to mankind, but I can at least assure you that you are doing more for me than if you had settled my accounts with Messrs. Cook & Sons, or Signora Vedova Paolini, my esteemed landlady. A writer who is worth anything accumulates more than he gives off, and never lives up to his income. His difficulty is the old one of digestion, Italian Art being as crucial for the Modern as Ital-ian cookery. Crucial indeed ! for diverse are the ways of the Hyperboreans cheek by jowl with *asciutta* and Tuscan table-wine, as any *osteria* will convince you. To one

man the oil is a delight : he will soak himself in it till his thought swims viscid in his
pate. To another it is abhorrent: straightway he calls for his German vinegar and
drowns the native flavour in floods as bitter
as polemics. Your wine too ! Overweak
for water, says one, who consumes a stout
fiaschone and spends a stertorous afternoon
in headache and cursing at the generous
home-grown. *Frizzante !* cries your next
to all his gods ; and flushes poison with
infected water. Crucial enough. So with
Art. Goethe went to Assisi.

" I left on my left," says he, " the vast mass of churches,
piled Babel-wise one over another—in one of which rest
the remains of the Holy Saint Francis of Assisi—with
aversion, for I thought to myself that the people who
assembled in them were mostly of the same stamp with
my captain and travelling companion."

Truly an odd ground of aversion to a
painted church that there might be a con-
fessional-box in the nave! But he had no
eyes for Gothic, being set on the Temple
of Minerva. The Right Honourable Joseph
Addison's views of Siena will be familiar
to you; but an earlier still was our excellent Mr. John Evelyn doing the grand tour;
going to Pisa, but seeing no frescos in the

Campo Santo; going to Florence, but seeing neither Santa Croce nor Santa Maria
Novella; in his whole journey he would
seem to have found no earlier name than
Perugino's affixed to a picture. Goethe
was urbane to Francia, "a very respect-
able artist"; he was astonished at Mantegna, "one of the older painters," but
accepted him as leading up to Titian : and
so—"thus was art developed after the
barbarous period." But Goethe had the
sweeping sublimity of youth with him.
"I have now seen but two Italian cities,
and for the first time; and I have spoken
with but few persons; and yet I know my
Italians pretty well!" Seriously, where in
criticism do you learn of an earlier painter
than Perugino, until you come to our day ?
And where now do you get the raptures
over the Carracci and Domenichino and
Guercino and the rest of them which the
last century expended upon their unthrifty
soil? Ruskin found Botticelli; yes, and
Giotto. Roscoe never so much as men-
tions either. Why should he, honest man ?
They could n't draw! Cookery is very
like Art, as Socrates told Gorgias. Un-
fortunately, it is far easier to verify your

impressions in the former case than in the latter. Yet that is the first and obvious duty of the critic—that is, the writer whomsoever. In my degree it has been mine. Wherefore, if I unfold anything at all, it shall not be the *Cicerone* nor the veiled "Anonymous," nor the *Wiederbelebung,* nor (I hope) the *Mornings in Florence,* but that thing in which you place such touching reliance—myself and my poor sensations. *Ecco !* I have nothing else. You take a boy out of school; you set him to book-reading, give him Shakespeare and a Bible, set him sailing in the air with the poets; drench him with painter's dreams *via* Titian's carmine and orange, Veronese's rippling brocades, Umbrian morning skies, and Tuscan hues wrought of moonbeams and flowing water—anon you turn him adrift in Italy, a country where all poets' souls seem to be caged in crystal and set in the sun, and say — "Here, dreamer of dreams, what of the day ?" *Madonna !* You ask and you shall obtain. I proceed to expand under your benevolent eye.

To me, Italy is not so much a place where pictures have been painted (some of which remain to testify), as a place where pictures have been lived and built; I fail to see how Perugia is not a picture by, say, Astorre Baglione. Perhaps I should be nearer the mark if I said it was a frozen epic. What I mean is, that in Italy it is still impossible to separate the soul and body of the soil, to say, as you may say in London or Paris,—here behind this sordid grey mask of warehouses and suburban villas lurks the soul that once was Shakespeare or once was Villon. You will not say that of Florence ; you will hardly say it (though the time is at hand) of Milan and Rome. Do the gondoliers still sing snatches of Ariosto? I don't know Venice. M. Bourget assures me his *vetturino* quoted Dante to him between Monte Pulciano and Siena; and I believe him. At any rate, in Italy as I have found it, the inner secret of Italian life can be read, not in painting alone, nor poem alone, but in the swift sun, in the streets and shrouded lanes, in the golden pastures, in the plains and blue mountains; in flowery cloisters and carved church porches—out of doors as well as in. The story of Troy is immortal—why not because the Trojans themselves live immor-

tal in their fabled sons ? That being so, I by no means promise you my sensations to be of the ear-measuring, nose-rubbing sort now so popular. I am bad at dates and soon tire of symbols. My theology may be to seek; you may catch me as much for the world as for Athanase. With world and doctor I shall, indeed, have little enough to do, for wherever I go I shall be only on the lookout for the soul of this bright-eyed people, whom, being no Goethe, I do not profess to understand or approve. Must the lover do more than love his mistress, and weave his sonnets about her white brows? I may see my mistress Italy embowered in a belfry, a fresco, the scope of a piazza, the lilt of a *stornello,* the fragrance of a legend. If I don't find a legend to hand I may, as lief as not, invent one. It shall be a legend fitted close to the soul of a fact, if I succeed: and if I fail, put me behind you and take down your four volumes of Rio, or your four-and-twenty of Rosini. Go to Crowe and Cavalcaselle and be wise! Parables !—I like the word—to go round about the thing, whose heart I cannot hit with my small arm, marking the goodly

masses and unobtrusive meek beauties of
it, and longing for them in vain. No
amount of dissecting shall reveal the core
of Sandro's Venus. For after you have
pared off the husk of the restorer, or bled
in your alembic the very juices the crafts-
man conjured withal, you come down to
the seamy wood, and Art is gone. Nay,
but your Morelli, your Crowe, ciphering as
they went for want of thought, what did
they do but screw Art into test-tubes, and
serve you up the fruit of their litmus-paper
assay with vivacity, may be,—but with
what kinship to the picture ? I maintain
that the peeling and gutting of fact must
be done in the kitchen: the king's guests
are not to know how many times the
cook's finger went from cate to mouth
before the seasoning was proper to the
table. The king is the artist, you are the
guest, I am the abstractor of quintessences,
the cook. Remember, the cook had not the
ordering of the feast : that was the king's
business—mine is to mingle the flavours
to the liking of the guest that the dish be
worthy the conception and the king's
honour.

Nor will I promise you that I shall not

break into a more tripping stave than our prose can afford, here and there. The pilgrim, if he is young and his shoes or his belly pinch him not, sings as he goes, the very stones at his heels (so music-steeped is this land) setting him the key. Jog the foot-path way through Tuscany in my company, it's Lombard Street to my hat I charm you out of your lassitude by my open humour. Things I say will have been said before, and better; my tunes may be stale and my phrasing rough: I may be irrelevant, irreverent, what you please. Eh, well! I am in Italy,—the land of shrugs and laughing. Shrug me (or my book) away; but, pray Heaven, laugh! And, as the young are always very wise when they find their voice and have their confidence well put out to usury, laugh (but in your cloak) when I am sententious or apt to tears. I have found *lacrimæ rerum* in Italy as elsewhere; and sometimes Life has seemed to me to sail as near to tragedy as Art can do. I suppose I must be a very bad Christian, for I remain sturdily an optimist, still convinced that it is good for us to be here, while the sun is up. Men and pictures, poems, cities, churches, comely deeds, grow like cabbages; they are of the soil, spring from it to the sun, glow open-hearted while he is there; and when he goes, they go. So grew Florence, and Shakespeare, and Greek myth—the three most lovely flowers of Nature's seeding I know of. And with the flowers grow the weeds. My first weed shall sprout by Arno, in a cranny of the Ponte Vecchio, or cling like a Dryad of the wood to some gnarly old olive on the hillside of Arcetri. If it bear no little gold-seeded flower, or if its pert leaves don't blush under the sun's caress, it sha n't be my fault or the sun's.

Take, then, my watered wine in the name of the Second Maccabæan, for here, as he says, "will I make an end. And if I have done well, and as is fitting the story, it is that which I desired: but if slenderly and meanly, it is that which I could attain unto."

I have killed you at the first cast. I feel it. Has any city, save, perhaps, Cairo, been so written out as Florence? I hear you querulous; you raise your eyebrows; you sigh as you watch the tottering ash of your second cigar. Mrs. Brown comes to tell you it is late. I agree with you quickly.

TOSCANELLA

Florence has often been sketched before—
putting Browning aside with his astounding
fresco-music—by Ruskin and George Eliot
and Mr. Henry James, to name only masters. But that is no reason why I should
not try my prentice hand. Florence alters
not at all. Men do. My picture, poor as
you like, shall be my own. It is not their
Florence or yours,—and, remember, I would
strike at Tuscany through Florence, and
throughout Tuscany keep my eye in her
beam,—but my own mellow kingcup of a
town, the glowing heart of the whole Arno
basin, whose suave and weather-warmed
grace I shall try to catch and distil. But
Mrs. Brown is right; it is late: the huntsmen
are up in America, as your good kinsman
has it, and I would never have you act your
own Antipodes. Addio.

I

EYE OF ITALY [1]

I HAVE been here a few days only—perhaps a week; if it's impressionism
you're after, the time is now or a year
hence. For, in these things of three stages,
two may be tolerable: the first clouding of
the water with the wine's red fire, or the
final resolution of the two into one humane
consistence; the intermediate course is, like
all times of process, brumous and hesitant.
After a dinner in the white piazza, shrinking slowly to blue under the keen young
moon's eye, watched over jealously by the
frowning bulk of Brunelleschi's globe—
after a dinner of *pasta con brodo,* veal cut-
lets, olives, and a bottle of right *Barbèra,*
let me give you a pastel (this is the medium
for such evanescences) of Florence herself.
At present I only feel. No one should think
—few people can—after dinner. Be patient
therefore; suffer me thus far.

[1] My thanks are due to the editor of *Black and White*
for permission to reprint the substance of this essay.

I would spare you, if I might, the horrors of my night-long journey from Milan. There is little romance in a railway: the novelists have worked it dry. That is, however, a part of my sum of perceptions which began, you may put it, at the dawn which saw Florence and me face to face. So I must in no wise omit it.

I find, then, that Italian railway-carriages are constructed for the convenience of luggage, and that passengers are an afterthought, as dogs or grooms are with us, to be suffered only if there be room, and on condition they look after the luggage. In my case we had our full complement of the staple; nevertheless, every passenger assumed the god, keeping watch on his traps, and thinking to shake the spheres at every fresh arrival. Thoughtless behaviour! for there were thus twelve people packed into a rocky landscape of cardboard portmanteaus and umbrella-peaks; twenty-four legs, and urgent need of stretching-room as the night wore on. There was jostling, there was asperity from those who could sleep and from those who would; there was more when two shock-head drovers—like First and Second Murderers in a tragedy

—insisted on taking off their boots. It was not that there was little room for boots; indeed I think they nursed them on their thin knees. It was at any rate too much even for an Italian passenger; for—well, well! their way had been a hot and a dusty one, poor fellows. So the guard was summoned, and came with all the implicit powers of a uniform and, I believe, a sword. The boots were strained on sufficiently to preserve the amenities of the way; they could not, of course, be what they had been; the carriage was by this a forcing-house. And through the long night we ached away an intolerable span of time with, for under-current, for sinister accompaniment to the pitiful strain, the muffled interminable plodding of the engine, and the rack of the wheels pulsing through space to the rhythm of some music-hall jingle heard in snatches at home. At intervals came shocks of contrast when we were brought suddenly face to face with a gaunt and bleached world. Then we stirred from our stupor, and sat looking at each other's stale faces. We had shrieked and clanked our way into some great naked station, shivering raw and cold under the electric lights, streaked with black shadows on its whitewash and patched with coarse advertisements. The porters' voices echoed in the void, shouting "*Piacenza*," "*Parma*," "*Reggio*," "*Modena*," "*Bologna*," with infinite relish for the varied hues of the final *a*. One or two cowed travellers slippered up responsive to the call, and we, the veterans who endured, set our teeth, shuddered, and smoked feverish cigarettes on the platform among the carriage-wheels and points; or, if we were new hands, watched awfully the advent of another sleeping train, as dingy as our own—yet a hero of romance! For it bore the hieratic and tremendous words, "*Roma, Firenze, Milano.*" It was privileged then; it ministered in the sanctuary. We glowed in our sordid skins, and could have kissed the foot-boards that bore the dust of Rome. I will swear I shall never see those three words printed on a carriage without a thrill. *Roma, Firenze, Milano,* — Lord! what a traverse.

Or we held long, purposeless rests at small wayside places where no station could be known, and the shrouded land stretched away on either side, not to be seen, but rather felt, in the cool airs that blew in, and the rustling of secret trees near by. No further sound was, save the muttered talking of the guards without and the simmering of the engine, on somewhere in front. And then *" Partenza ! "* rang out in the night, and *" Pronti ! "* came as a faint echo on before. We laboured on, and the dreams began where they had broken off. For we dreamed in these times, fitful and lurid, coloured dreams; flashes of horrible crises in one's life; interminable precipices; a river skiff engulfed in a swirl of green sea-water; agonies of repentance; shameful failure, defeat, memories—and then the steady pulsing of the engine, and thick, impermeable darkness choking up the windows again. How I ached for the dawn !

I awoke from what I believe to have been a panic of snoring, to hear the train clattering over the sleepers and points, and to see—oh, human, brotherly sight !— the broad level light of morning stream out of the east. We were stealing into a city asleep. Tall flat houses rose in the chill mist to our left and stared blankly down upon us with close-barred green eyelids.

Gas-lamps in swept streets flickered dirty yellow in the garish light. A great purple dome lay ahead, flanked by the ruddy roofs and gables of a long church. My heart leapt for Florence. Pistoja!

And then, at Prato, a nut-brown old woman with a placid face got into our carriage with a basket of green figs and some

bottles of milk for the Florentine markets. So we were nearing. And soon we ran in between lines of white and pink villas edged with rows of planes drenched still with dews and the night mists, among bullock-carts and queer shabby little *vetture*, everything looking light and elfin in the brisk sunshine and autumn bite—into the barrel-like station, and I into the arms, say rather the arm-chair, of Signora Vedova

Paolini, chattiest and most motherly of landladies.

Earth, Air, Fire, Water, Florence, form the five elements of our planet according to the testimony of Boniface VIII. of clamant and not very Catholic memory. That is true if you take it this way. You cannot resolve an element; but you cannot resolve Florence; therefore Florence is an element. *Ecco!* She is like nothing else in Nature, or (which is much the same thing) Art. You can have olives elsewhere, and Gothic elsewhere; you can have both at Arles, for instance. You can have *campanili* printed white (but not rose-and-white, not rose-and-gold-and-white) on blue anywhere along the Mediterranean from Tripoli to Tangier: you will find Giotto at Padua, and statues growing in the open air at Naples. But for the silvery magic of olives and blue; for a Gothic which has the supernatural and always restless eagerness of the North, held in check, reduced to our level by the blessedly human sanity of Romanesque; for sculpture which sprouts from the crumbling church-sides like some frankly happy stonecrop, or wallflower, just as wholesomely coloured and tenderly shaped, you must come to Florence. Come for choice in this golden afternoon of the year. Green figs are twelve-a-penny; you can get peaches for the asking, and grapes and melons without it; brown men are treading the wine-fat in every little white hill-town, and in Florence itself you may stumble upon them, as I once did, plying their mystery in a battered old church—sight only to be seen in Italy, where religions have been many, but religionists substantially the same. That is the Italian way; there was the practical evidence. Imagine the sight. A gaunt and empty old basilica, the beams of the rood still left, the dye of fresco still round the walls and tribune—here the dim figure of Sebastian roped to his tree, there the cloudy forms of Apostles or the Heavenly Host shadowed in masses of crimson or green—and, down below, a slippery purple sea, frothed sanguine at the edges, and wild, half-naked creatures treading out the juice, dancing in the oozy stuff rhythmically, to the music of some wailing air of their own. *Saturnia regna* indeed, and in the haunt of Sant' Ambrogio, or under the hungry eye of San Bernardino, or other lean ascetic of the Middle Age. But that, after all, is Italian, not necessarily Florentine or Tuscan. I must needs abstract the unique quintessential humours of this my eye of Italy. Stendhal, do you remember? did n't like one of these. He said that in Florence people talked about "huesta hasa" when they would say "questa casa," and thus turned Italian into a mad Arabic. So they do, especially the women: why not? The poor Stendhal loved Milan, wrote himself down "Arrigo Milanese"—and what can you expect from a Milanese?

They tell me, who know Florence well, that she is growing unwieldy. Like a bulky old *concierge,* they say, she sits in the passage of her Arno, swollen, fat, and featureless, a kind of Chicago, a city of tame conveniences ungraced by arts. That means that there are suburbs and tramways; it means that the gates will not hold her in; it has a furtive stab at the railway station and the omnibus in the Piazza del Duomo: it is *Mornings in Florence.* The suggestion is that Art is some pale remote virgin who must needs shiver and withdraw at the touch of actual life : the art-lover must maunder over his mistress's wrongs instead of manfully insisting upon her rights, her

everlasting triumphant justifications. Why
this watery talk of an Art that was and may
not be again, because we go to bed by
electricity and have our hair brushed by
machinery? Pray has Nature ceased? or
Life? Art will endure with these fine things,
which in Florence, let me say, are very fine
indeed. But there 's a practical answer to
the indictment. As a city she is a mere
cupful. You can walk from Cantagalli's,
at the Roman Gate, to the Porta San Gallo,
at the end of the Via Cavour, in half the
time it would take you to go from New-
gate to Kensington Gardens. Yet whereas
in London such a walk would lead you
through a slice of a section, in Florence
you would cut through the whole city
from hill to hill. You are never away from
the velvet flanks of the Tuscan hills. Every
street-end smiles an enchanting vista upon
you. Houses frowning, machicolated and
sombre, or gay and golden-white with cool
green jalousies and spreading eaves, stretch
before you through mellow air to a distance
where they melt into hills, and hills into
sky; into sky so clear and rarely blue, so
virgin pale at the horizon, that the hills
sleep brown upon it under the sun, and the

cypresses, nodding a-row, seem funeral weeds beside that radiant purity. Some such adorable stretch of tilth and pasture, sky and cloud, hangs like a god's crown beyond the city and her towers. In the long autumn twilight Fiesole and the hills lie soft and purple below a pale green sky. There is a pause at this time when the air seems washed for sleep—every shrub, every feature of the landscape is cut clean as with a blade. The light dies, the air deepens to wet violet, and the glimpses of the hill-town gleam like snow. At such times Samminiato looms ghostly upon you and fades slowly out. The flush in the East faints and fails and the evening star shines like a gem. It is hot and still in the broad Piazza Santa Maria ; they are lighting the lamps; the swarm grows of the eager, shabby, spendthrift crowd of young Italians, so light-hearted and fluent, and so prodigal of this old Italy of theirs—and ours. All this I have been watching as I might. Nature clings to the city, playing her rhythmic dance at the end of every street.

Nature clings. Yes; but she is within as well as without. What is that sentimental platitude of somebody's (the worst kind of platitude, is it not?) about the sun being to flowers what Art is to Life? It has the further distinction of being untrue. In Florence you learn that what he is to flowers, that he is to Art. For I soberly believe that under his rays Florence has grown open like some rare white water-lily; that sun and sky have set the conditions, struck, as it were, the chord. I have wandered through and through her recessed ways the length of this bright and breezy October week; and have marked where I walked the sun's great hand laid upon palace and cloister and bell-tower. He has summoned up these flat-topped houses, these precipitous walls beneath which winds the darkened causeway. One seems to be travelling in a mountain gorge with, above, a thin ribbon of sky, fluid blue, flawless of cloud, like the sea. He, that so masterful sun, has given Florence the apathetic, beaten aspect of a southern town; he and the temperate sky have fixed the tone for ever; and the nimble air—"nimbly and sweetly" recommending itself—has given the quaintness and the freaksomeness of the North. This bursts out, young and irresponsible, in pinnacle, crocket, and gable, in towers

like spears, and in the eager lancet windows which peer upwards out of Orsammichele and the Dominican church. This
mixture is Florence and has made her art.
The blue of the sky gives the key to her
palette, the breath of the west wind, the
salt wind from our own Atlantic, tingles in
her *campanili;* and the Italian sun washes
over all with his lazy gold. Habit and inclination both speak. She rejects no wise
thing and accepts every lovely thing. Nature and Art have worked hand in hand, as
they will when we let them. For what is
an art so inimitable, so innocent, so intimate as this of Tuscany, after all, but a high
effort of creative Nature—*Natura naturans,*
as Spinosa calls her? Here, on the weather-
fretted walls, a Della Robbia blossoms out
in natural colours—blue and white and
green. They are Spring's colours. You
need not go into the Bargello to understand
Luca and Andrea at their happy task; as
well go to a botanical museum to read the
secret of April. See them on the dusty
wall of Orsammichele. They have wrought
the blossom of the stone—clusters of bright-
eyed flowers with the throats and eyes of
angels, singing, you might say, a children's

24

EARTHWORK

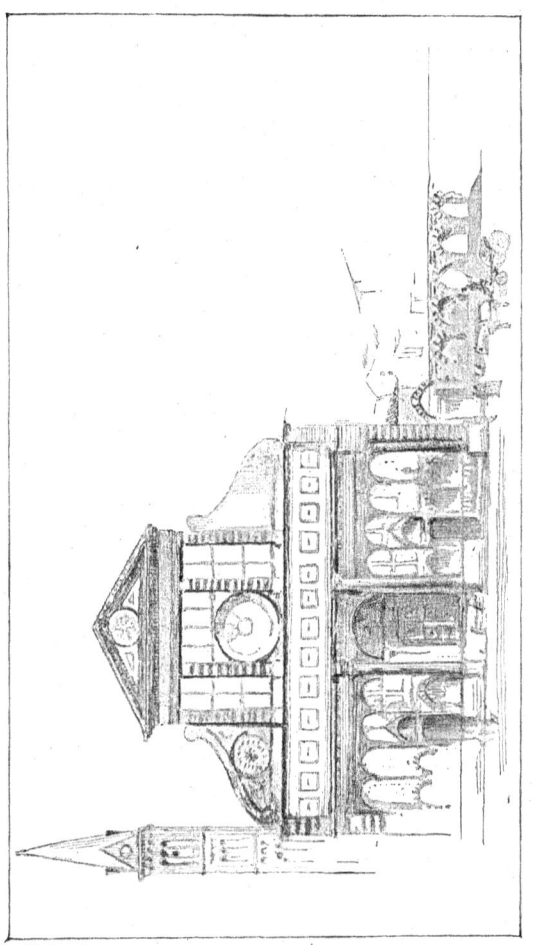

THE DOMINICAN CHURCH

hymn to Our Lady, throned and pure in the midst of the bevy. See the Spedale degli Innocenti, where a score of little flowery white children grow, open-armed, out of their sky-blue medallions. Really, are they lilies, or children, or the embodied strophes of a psalter? you ask. I mix my metaphors like an Irishman, but you will see my meaning. All the arts blend in art: "Rien ne fait mieux entendre combien un faux sonnet est ridicule que de s'imaginer une femme ou une maison faite sur ce modèle-là." Pascal knew; and so did Philip Sidney. "Nature never set forth the earth in so rich tapestry as divers poets have done"; and the nearer truth seems to be that Art is Nature made articulate, Nature's soul inflamed with love and voicing her secrets through one man to many. So there may be no difference between me and a cabbage-rose but this, that I can consider my own flower, how it grows, or rather, when it is grown.

It is very pleasant sometimes to think that wistful guess of Plato's true in spite of everything—that the state is the man grown great, as the universe is the state grown infinite. It explains that Florence has a soul, the broader image of her sons', and that this soul speaks in Art, utters itself in flower of stone and starry stretches of fresco (like that serene blue and grey band in the Sistine chapel which redeems so many of Rome's waste places), sings colour-songs (there are such affairs) on church and cloister walls. Seeing these good things, we should rather hear the town's voice crying out her fancy to friendly hearts. Thus—let me run the figure to death—if Luca's blue-eyed medallions are the crop of the wall, they are also the soul of Florence, singing a blithe secular song about gods whose abiding charm is the art that made them live. And if the towers and domes are the statelier flowers, of the garden, lily, hollyhock, tulip of the red globe, so they are Florence again as she strains forward and up, sternly defiant in the Palazzo Vecchio, bright and curious at Santa Croce, pure, chaste as a seraph, when, thrilling with the touch of Giotto, she gazes in the clarity of her golden and rosy marbles, tinted like a pearl and shaped like an arch-angel, towards the blue vault whose eye she is.

Wandering, therefore, through this high

26

city; loitering on the bridge whereunder
turbid Arno glitters like brass; standing by
the yellow Baptistery; or seeing in Santa
Croce cloister—where I write these lines—
seven centuries of enthusiasm mellowed
down by sun and wind into a comely
dotage of grey and green, one is disposed
to wonder whether we are only just beginning to understand Art, or to misunder-
stand it? Has the world slept for two
thousand years? Is Degas the first artist?
Was Aristotle the first critic, and is Mr.
George Moore the second? As a white
pigeon cuts the blue, and every pinion of
him shines as burnished agate in the live
air, things shape themselves somewhat. I
begin to see that Art *is*, and that men have
been, and shall be, but never *are*. Facts
are an integral part of life, but they are not
life. I heard a metaphysician say once that
matter was the adjective of life, and thought
it a mighty pretty saying. In a true sense,
it would seem, Art is that adjective. For
so surely as there are honest men to insist
how true things are or how proper to
moralising, there will be Art to sing how
lovely they are, and what amiable dwell-
ings for us. Thus fortified, I think I can

understand Magister Joctus Fiorentiæ. He
lies behind these crumbling walls. Traces
of his crimson and blue still stain the cloister-walk. What was he telling us in crimson and blue? How dumb Zacharias spelt
out the name of his son John in the roll of
a book? Hardly that, I think.

II

LITTLE FLOWERS

THE Via del Monte alle Croce is a leafy
way cut between hedgerows, in the
morning time heavy with dew and the
smell of wet flowers. Where it strays out
of the Gira al Monte there is a crumbly
brick wall, a well, and a little earthen
shrine to Madonna—a daub, it is true, of
glaring chromes and blues, thick in glaze
and tawdry devices of stout Cupids and
roses, but somehow, on this suggestive
Autumn morning, innocent and blue of eye
as the carolling throngs of Luca which it
travesties. And a pious inscription cut below testifieth how Saint Francis, "in
friendly talk with the Blessed Mariano di
Lugo," paused here before it, and then
vanished. It is not necessary to believe in
ghosts; but I'll go bail that story is true.
We are but two stones' throw from the
gaunt hulk of a Franciscan church; a file
of dusty cypresses marks the ruins of a
painful Calvary cut in the waste and shale

of the hill-side. Below, as in a green pasture, Florence shines like a dove's egg in her nest of hills ; I can pick out among the sheaf of spears which hedge her about the daintiest of them all, the crocketed pinnacle of Santa Croce, grey on blue; and then the lean ridge of a shrine the barest, simplest, and most honest in all Tuscany. Certainly Saint Francis, "familiarmente discorrendo," appeared in this place. I need no reference to the Annals of the Seraphic Order—part, book, and page—to convince me. My stone gives them. "Ann. Ord. Min. Tom. cclii. fasc. 3," and so on. That is but a sorry concession to our short-sightedness. For if we believe not the shrine which we have seen, how shall we believe Giotto? What of Giotto? That is my point.

Something too much, it may be, of modern art-criticism, which is ashamed of thinking, snuffeth at pictures which tell you things, at literature in books or music or church ornament. Is literature not good anywhere? Have we exhausted the *Arabian Nights* or the *Acta Sanctorum*? At any rate, if we must choose between Giotto and the prophet of the *Yellow Book,* my heart is fixed. I am for the teller of tales. Story-telling it is, glorification of one whom Mr. George Moore would call (has, indeed, called) a " squint-eyed Italian Saint "—and whether he objected to malformity, nationality or calling, I never could learn— this too it may be; it may tend to edification and I know not what beside. I will grant all that. And though it is hard to prophesy what might have happened five hundred years ago ; though there might have been a Giotto without a Francis of whom to speak; yet I never knew a case where a painter (call him poet if you will; he will be none the worse for that) fell so directly into the gap awaiting him. The Gospel living and tangible again ! Spirits, apparitions, as of three mysterious sisters, met you in the open country, and crying "Hail! Lady Poverty," straightly vanished. A legend was a-making round about the strange life not fifty years closed, a life which seems, extravagance apart, to have been a lyrical outburst, a strophe in the hymn of praise which certain happy people were singing just then. It was a *Gloria in Excelsis* for a second time in Christian Annals which did not end in a wail of " Agnus Dei, qui tollis peccata, miserere." Why should it ? Should the children of the bride-chamber fast when the bridegroom was with them ? And of all the "wreath'd singers at the marriage-door," blithest and sanest was Master Joctus of Florence. This being so, I hope I shall not be accused of any mischief if I say that in Giotto I see one of the select company of immortals whose work can never be surpassed because it is entirely adequate to the facts and atmosphere he selected. The standard of a work of art must always be—Is it well done ? rather than—Is it well intentioned ? Wherefore, if Giotto or anybody else choose to spend himself upon a sermon or an essay or an article of the Creed, and do well thereby, I may not blame him, nor call him back to study the play of light across a marsh or the flight of pigeons in the westering sun. "Ma, basta, basta così," you may say with the Cavaliere of Goldoni.

Santa Croce church is of the barrack-room stamp, dim and enormous, grey with years and seamed with work. Its impressiveness (for with Orvieto and a fleet of churches at Ravenna it stands above all Italy in that) consists mainly, I believe, in its being built of exactly the moral bones of the religion it was intended to embody. An Italian religion, namely ; perfectly sane, at bottom practical, with a base of plain, every-day, ten-commandment morality. That was the base of Saint Francis' good brown life : therefore Santa Croce is admirably built, squared, mortised, and compacted by skilled workmen to whom bricklaying was a fine art. But, withal, this religion had its lyric raptures, its "In fuoco Amor mi mise," or its sobbing at the feet of the Cruci-fied, its *Corotto* and Seven Sorrowful Mys-teries : accordingly Santa Croce, like a pollarded lime, reserves its buds, harbours and garners them, throws out no suckers or lateral adornments the length of its trunk, but bursts into a flowery crown of them at the top—a whole row of chapels

3

along the cross-beam of the *tau;* and in the place of honour a shallow apse pierced with red lancets and aglow like an opal. Never a chapel of them but is worth study and a stiff neck. After the Rule came the *Fioretti ;* after Francis and Bonaventure came Celano and Jacopone da Todi ; after Arnolfo del Lapo and his attention to business came the hours of ease when he planned the airy plume on which the church leaps skyward; and came also Giotto to weave the crown of Santa Croce.

I take the Tuscan nature to be so constituted that it will play with any given subject of speculation in much the same way. With one or two mighty exceptions to be sure—Dante, of course, Buonarroti, of course, and, for all his secularities, Boccace—it is not imagination you find in Tuscany. Rather, it is a sweet and delicate, a wholesome, a home-grown fancy, wantoning with thought which may be unpleasant, unhealthy, grave, frivolous— what you will ; yet playing in such a way, and with such intuitive taste and breeding that no harm ensues nor any nausea. They realise for me a fairy country ; I can think no evil of a Tuscan. So I can read Boccace

THE ETERNAL CHILD

the infidel, Poggio the gross, where Voltaire makes me a bigot and Catulle Mendès ashamed. The fresh breeze blowing through the *Decameron* keeps the air sweet. Even Lorenzo is a child for me, and Macchiavel, " the man without a soul," I decline to take seriously. Consider, then, all Tuscan art from this point of view, the weaving of innocent fancies round some chance-caught theme. Christianity may have been the *point d'appui*. No doubt it generally was. What then ? Have you never heard two children dreaming aloud of the ways of God, or the troubles of Christ ? How they humanise, how they realise the Mystery ! Just such a pretty babble I find in the Spanish chapel, which to take in any other spirit would work a madness in the brain. You remember the North wall, apotheosis of Saint Thomas and what-not, for all the world like a paradigm of the irregular verb " Aquinizo." What are we to suppose Lippo Memmi (or whoever else it was) to have been about when he hung in mid-air on his swinging bridge and stained the wet square red and green ? To read Ruskin you would think he was fulminating *urbi et orbi* with the

Summa or *Cur Deus homo* at his fingers'
ends. Depend upon it he was doing quite
other, or the artistic temper (phrase rend-
ered loathsome by the halfpenny newspapers) suffered a relapse between the days
of King David and the days of his brother
Lippo Lippi. Are we to suppose that a
man who could live in intimate commerce
with fourteen such gracious ladies as he
has set there, ranged on their carved *sedilia*
—his Britomart trim and debonnaire; his
willowy Carità ; his wimpled matron in
clean white who masquerades as I know
not what branch of theology ; his pretty
girlish Geometry of coiled and braided hair
and the yet unloosed girdle of demure vir-
ginity ; his maid Musica crowned with
roses, and Logica, the bold-eyed and
open-throated wench, hand to hip—is this
the man for sententiousness ? Out, out !
Could anyone save a humourist of high
order have given Moses such a pair of
horns, or set, under Music, such a shagged
Tubal to belabour an anvil ? The wall
sings like an anthology,—a Gothic anthology where "Bele Aliz matin leva" is
versicle, and "In un boschetto trovai pas-
torella" antiphon. You might as well talk

of Christian Mathematics as of Christian Art, or bind the sweet influences of Pleiades as the volant sallies of a poet's wit.

Once we get it into our heads that the Tuscans were fanciful children, always, and the discrepancy of critics, of Ruskin and Mr. George Moore, of Rio and Mr. Addington Symonds, may vanish. For another thing, we shall understand and allow for the standard of Santa Croce and the *Fioretti*. From the latter nosegay I take this :

" It happened one day as Brother Peter was standing to his prayer, thinking earnestly about the Passion of Christ, how the blessed Mother of him, and John Evangelist his best-beloved, and Saint Francis too, were painted at the foot of the Cross, crucified indeed with him through anguish of the mind, that there came upon him the longing to know which of these three had endured the bitterest pains of that anguish, the Mother who bore our Lord, or the Disciple familiar to his bosom, or Saint Francis crucified also even as he was. And as he stood thinking on these things, lo ! there appeared before him the Virgin Mary with Saint John Evangelist and Saint Francis, robed in splendid apparel and of glory wonderful; but Saint Francis' robe was more cunningly wrought than Saint John's. Now Peter stood quite scared at the sight ; but Saint John bade him take comfort, saying, ' Be not afraid, dearest brother, for we are come hither to dispel thy doubt. You are to know, then, that above all creatures the Mother of Christ and I grieved over the Passion of our Lord. But since that day Saint

Francis has felt more anguish than any other. Therefore, as you see, he is in glory now.' Then Brother
Peter asked him, and said, ' Most holy Apostle of Christ,
wherefore cometh it that the vesture of Saint Francis is
more glorious than thine ? ' Answered him Saint John,
' The reason is this, for that when he was in the world
he wore a viler than ever I did.' So then Saint John
gave him a vestment which he carried on his arm, and
the holy company vanished."

This, be sure, is true ; and I have its English parallel ready to hand. For I once
heard a father and his child talking of the
goodness of God. "God," says the father,
" gives thee the milk to thy porridge " ; and
the child thought it a good saying, yet
puzzled over it, doubting, as it afterwards
appeared, the part to be assigned to a friend
of his, the daily milkman. And so he
solved it. "God makes the milk and the
milkman brings it," he said. The *Fioretti*,
if you must needs break a butterfly on your
dissecting-board, was written, as I judge,
by a bare-foot Minorite of forty ; compiled,
that is, from the wonderings, the pretty
adjustments and naïve disquisitions of any
such weather-worn brown men as you may
see to-day toiling up the Calvary to their
Convent. And in this same story-telling
Giotto is an adept. He loves to gather his

fellows round him and speak of Saints and Archangels, where our youngsters talk of fairy godmothers and white rabbits. To say this is not Art, as the critics profanely teach, is monstrous. Is not the *Fioretti* literature, or the Gospel according to Saint Luke literature? And is not Religion the highest art of all, the large elementary poetry at the core of the heart of man? Just so was the craft which disposed the rings of that wonderful ornament round about the Bardi chapel, rings of clean arabesque wrought in line upon pale blue and pink and brown, and which in so doing fitted the Franciscan thaumaturgy with an exact garment tenderly adjusted to every wave of its abandonment—even so was this a great art indeed. For you ask of an art no more than this, that it shall be adequately representative : there are no comparative degrees.

So when I learn from the works of Ruskin that he can "read a picture to you as, if Mr. Spurgeon knew anything about art, Mr. Spurgeon would read it,—that is to say, from the plain, common-sense Protestant side " ; or when I learn from the works of Mr. George Moore that Sir Frederick Burton

made of the National Gallery a Museum ;
or when one complains of a picture that it
is not didactic, and another that it holds a
thought, I make haste to laugh lest I should
do wrong to Tuscany, that looked upon the
world to love it : for she saw that it was
very good.

III

A SACRIFICE AT PRATO

(An old-fashioned narrative)*

THE rim of the sun was burning the hill tops, and already the vanguard of his strength stemming the morning mists, when I and my companion first trod the dust of a small town which stood in our path. It still lay very hard and white, however, and sharply edged to its girdle of olives and mulberry trees drenched in dews, a compactly folded town well fortified by strong walls and many towers, with the mist upon it and softly over it like a veil. For it lay well under the shade of the hills awaiting the sun's coming. In the streets, though they were by no means asleep, but, contrariwise, busy with the traffic of men and pack-mules, there was a shrewd bite

---

* Perhaps I may be allowed to explain that this article was written from the stand-point of a cultivated Pagan of the Empire, who should have journeyed in Time as well as Space.

as of night air ; looking up we could perceive how faint the blue of the sky was,
and the cloud-flaw how rosy yet with the
flush of Aurora's beauty-sleep. Therefore
we were glad to get into the market-place,
filled with people and set round with goodly
brick buildings, and to feel the light and
warmth steal about our limbs.

"It would seem fitting," said I, "seeing
that day is at hand and already we enjoy
the first-fruits of his largess, that we should
seek some neighbouring shrine where we
might praise the gods. For never yet was
land that had not, as its fairest work, gods :
and in a land so fair as this there must
needs be gods yet fairer, and shrines to case
them in." This I said, having observed
pious offerings laid upon the shrines of
divers gods by the road. At the which,
looking curiously, it seemed to me that the
inhabitants of this country were favoured
above the common with devout thoughts
and the objects of them—gods and goddesses. You might not pass a farm without its tutelary altar to the genius of the
place, some holy shade, or—as she was
figured as a matron—some great land-god-
dess, perhaps Cybele, or the Bona Dea ;

and pleasant it was to me to see that the tufts of common flowers set before her were for the most part smiling and fresh with the dew that assured an early gathering. In the streets of the city, moreover, I had seen many more such, slight affairs (it is true) of painted earthenware, some gaudily adorned with green and yellow colour and of workmanship as raw, some painted flat on the wall of a recess (in which was more skill, though the device was often gross enough—to dwell upon death and despair), and some again of choice beauty, both of form and colour, and a most rare blitheness, as it might be the spirit of the contrivers breaking through the hard stone. And all of these I knew to be gods, but the devices upon them were hard to be read, or approved. There was a naked youth pierced with arrows, wherein the texture of smooth flesh accorded not well with the bitterness of his hurt ; a young man also, bearded, of spare and mournful habit and girt with a rope round his middle ; in his hands were wounds, as again of arrows, and there was a rent in his garment where a javelin had torn a way into his side. Such suffering of wounds and broken flesh stared sharply up against the young flowers and grasses which spoke of healthy wind and rain and a sun-kissed earth. Goddesses also I saw—a virgin of comely red and white visage ; yellow-haired she was, crowned like a king's daughter ; at her side a wheel, cruelly spiked on the outer edge and not easily to be related to so heartsome a maid. But before them all (with one grim exception, to be sure) I saw the Earth-Mother who had been upon the farm and homestead-walls, of the same high perfection of form, and in raiment stately and adorned, yet (it would seem) something sorrowful as she might mourn the loss of lover or young child. Now the darkest sight I saw was that exception before rehearsed ; and it was this. A black cross stood in the most joyful places of the city, and one suffered upon it to very death. Whereat I marvelled greatly, saying, "Who is the man thus tormented whom the people worship as a god ?" And my companion answered,

"A great god he is, if the country report lie not, and has many names which amount to this, that he has freed this nation from bondage and died that he may live again, and they too. And of the truth of what they say I cannot speak ; but I think he is Bacchus the Redeemer, who, as you, Balbus, know, was no wanton reveller in lasciviousness, but a very god of great benevolence and of wisdom truly dark and awful. Who also took our mortal nature upon him and suffered in the shades : rising whence (for he was god and man) like the dawn from the night's bosom, or the flooding of spring weather from the iron gates of winter, he sped over land and sea, touching earth and the dwellers upon it. And to those he touched tongues were given and soothsaying, and to many the transports of inspiration and divine madness, as of poets and rhapsodists. And tragedy and choral odes are his, and the furious splendour of dances. But of the worship of Dionysus you know something, having been at Eleusis and beheld the holy mysteries.

" Now the god of this people has the same gift of tongues and madness of possession. To him are also sacred priests of the oracle, and high tragedies, and the wailing of music, and streaming processions of virgins and young boys. He too agonised and arose stronger and more shining than befcre, dying, indeed, and rising at the very vernal equinox we have mentioned. He too is worshipped in certain Mysteries whereat the confession of inquity and the cleansing of hearts come first: and the sacrifice is just that wheaten cake and fruit of the vine whereof, at Eleusis, you have praised to me the simplicity and ethic beauty. And he can inspire his devotees with frenzy. For I have heard that certain men of the country, on a day, and urged by his dæmon, run naked from place to place in honour of him, lashing their bare backs with ox-goads; and will fast by the week together, they and the women alike ; and that pious virgins, under stress of these things, swoon and are floated betwixt earth and heaven, and afterwards relate their blissful encounters and prophesy strange matters; receiving also dolorous wounds (which nevertheless are very sweet to them) like to the wounds which he himself received unto death; and all these things they endure because they are mystically fraught with the wisdom and efficacy of the god. Nay, I have been told that in the parts over sea, towards the North and

West, he is worshipped, just as at Eleusis,
with pipes and timbrels and brazen cymbals
and all excess of music ; and there they
dance in his service and suffer the ecstasies
of the Mænads and Corybants in the Diony-
siac revel. But this I find quaint to be
believed."

Now when I had heard so much, I was
the more desirous to find some temple
where I could observe the cult of this
wounded god, and so sought counsel of my
friend versed in the people's learning. To
my questioning he replied that it would be
easy. We were (said he) in the market-
place among the buyers and chafferers of
fruit, vegetables, earthenware, milk, eggs,
and such country produce; which honest
folk, it being the hour of the morning
sacrifice and the temple facing us, would
soon abandon their brisk toil for religion's
sake; whereupon we too would go. So I
looked across the square and saw a very
fair building, lofty and many windowed, all
of clean white marble, banded over with
bars of a smooth black stone, curiously
carved, moreover, in sculptured work of
gods and men and of flowers and fruits—
all cut in the pure marble. At one side was

a noble rostrum, of the like fine stone,
whereon young boys and girls, as it were
fauns and dryads and other woodland
creatures, capered as they list: and above
the midmost door a semi-circle of pale blue
enamel, whereon was the image of the
Great Goddess in gleaming white. She
was of smiling debonnair countenance and
in the full pride of her blossom-time—being
as a young woman whose girdle is new
loosed to the will of her lord—and in her
arms was a naked child, finely wrought to
the size of life. On either side of her a
beautiful youth (in whom I must needs
admire the smoothness of their chins and
the bravery of their vesture shining in the
clear light), did reverence to the Goddess
and the child: and there were beings,
winged like birds, with the faces of strong
boys, but no bodies at all that I could see,
who flew above them all. This was brave
work, very wonderful to me in a people
who, thus excellently inspired and having
such comely smiling divinities and so clear
a vision of them before their eyes, could
yet be curious after suffering heroes and
stabbed virgins and gods with mangled
limbs. But we went into the temple with

PRATO

the good people of the country-side to the sound of bells from a high tower hard by. And I was something surprised that they brought no beasts with them for the sacrifice, nor any of the fruits which were so abundant in the land ; but my companion reminded me again that the sacrifice was ready prepared within, and was, as it were, emblematical of all fruits and every sort of meat, being that wine and bread into which you may comprehend all bodily and (by a figure) ghostly sustenance. By this we were within the temple, which I now perceived was a pantheon, having altars to all the gods, some only of whose shrines I had remarked on the way thither. Dark and lofty it was, with piered arches that soared into the mist, and jewelled windows painfully worked in histories and fables of old time—all as far apart as conceivably might be from the holy places of my own country ; for whereas, with us, the level gaze of the sun is never absent, and through the colonnades you would see stretches of the far blue country, or, perchance, the shimmer of the restless sea, here no light of day could penetrate, and all the senses might apprehend must be of

4

solemn darkness, longing thoughts to cleave
it, and, afar off and dim, some flutter of
even light as of blest abodes. A strange
people ! to despise the sure and fair, for the
taunting shadows of desire. But, growing
more familiar in the middle of newness and
the awe that comes of it, I was again
amazed at the number of the gods, their
nature and sort. I saw again the arrow-
stricken youth, whom we call Asclepius
(but never knew thus tormented—as with
his father's arrows !) and again the Maid of
the Wheel, Fortune as I suppose: but with
us the wheel is not so manifestly bitter.
Then also the wounded hero, cowled and
corded, ragged exceedingly, the like of
whom we have not, unless it be some
stripling loved by an immortal and wounded
to death by grudging Fate, as Atys or
Adonis. And if, indeed, this were one of
them, the image-maker did surely err in
making him of so vile a presence—a thing
against all likelihood that the gods, being
themselves of super-excellent shapeliness,
should stoop to anything of less favour.
Yet he was of singular sweetness in his
pains, and high fortitude : and he was
much loved of the people, as I afterwards

learned. And one was a young knight, winged and with a sword in his hand ; at his feet a grievous worm of many folds. This I must take for Perseus but that his radiancy did rather point him for Phœbus, the lord of days and the red sun. But in the centre of the whole temple was an altar, high and broad, fenced about with steps and a rail, which I took to be made unto the god of gods or perhaps the king of that country, until I saw the black cross and the Agonist hanging from it as one dead. Then I knew that the chief god of this people was Dionysus the Redeemer, if it were really he. But I had reason to alter my opinion on that matter as you shall hear.

By this the temple was filled with the country folk who flocked in with the very reek of their toil upon them and hardly so much as their implements and marketable wares left behind. They were of all ages and conditions, both youths and maids, arrowy, tall, and open-eyed; and aged ones there were, bowed by labour and seamed with the stress of weather or the assaults of unstaying Fate : whereof, for the most part, the women sat down against

the wall and plied dextrously their fans ;
but the men stood leaning against the
pillars which held the timbers of the roof.
And they conversed easily together, and
some were merry, and others, as I could
perceive, beset with affairs of government
or business—for they talked more vehe-
mently of these matters than of others, as
men will, even beneath the very eyelids of
the god.   And so I could understand that
this sacrifice was not the yearly celebrating
of high mysteries, but the common piety
of every day with which it is rather seemly
than essential we should begin our labouring.   There were, indeed, signs in the
apparelling of the temple that more solemn
festivals were sometimes held, as the de-
livery of oracles, the calculation of auspices
and such like : that, at least, I took to be
the intention of small recesses along the
walls, that, through a grating of fine brass,
a priest of the sanctuary uttered the wisdom
of the god in sentences which the meaner
sort should fit with what ease they might
to their circumstances.   For, I suppose, it is
still found good that the dark saying of the
Oracle should be illumined by the subtlety
of the initiate and not by the necessities

of the simple. And while I was thus musing I found the ministrants in shining white about the great altar, busied with the preparation for the rite, lighting the torches (very inconsiderable for so large a building, but, mayhap, proportionate to the condition of the people) : and they placed a great book upon the altar, and bowed themselves ere they left. And soon afterwards, to the ringing of a bell, came the priest's boy carrying the offering of the altar, and the priest himself in stiff garments of white and yellow.

Now, for the sacrifice, I could not well understand it, save that it was very shortly done and with a light heart accepted by the people, who (I thought) held it as of the number of those services whose bare performance is efficacious and wholesome—on account, partly of reverent antiquity and long usage, and partly as having some hidden virtue best known to the god in whose honour it is done. For in my own country, I know well, there were many such rites, whose commission edified the people more than their omission would have dishonoured the god: wise men, therefore (as priests and philosophers), who would live in peace, bow their bodies by rule, knowing surely that their souls may be bolt upright notwithstanding. So here were many solemn acts which, doubtless, once had some now unfathomable design and purport, diligently rehearsed, while the worshippers gazed about with dull unconcern, or, being young, cast eyes of longing upon the country wenches set laughing and rosy by the wall, or, old, nursed their infirmities. And, on a sudden, a bell rang; and again rang; and the packed body of men and women fell upon their faces, and so remained in a horrific silence for a space where a man might count a score. Thereafter another bell, as of release. So the assembly rose to their feet and, as I saw, swept from their foreheads and breasts the dust of the temple floor. But as soon as it was over, a very old priest came through the press and offered the same sacrifice in a little guarded shrine at the lower end, amid many lamps and wax torches and glittering ornaments. Here was more devotion among the people, indeed a great struggling and elbowing just so as to touch the altar, or the steps of it, or the priest's hem, or even the rails which fenced the shrine.

And with some show of good reason was this hubbub, as I learned. For here was indeed treasured the Girdle of Venus (this being her very sanctuary) and as much desired as ever it was by women great with child or wanting to conceive. And I looked very curiously upon it, but the Girdle I could never see; only there was a painted image over the altar of the great queen-mother, Venus Genetrix herself, depicted as a broad-browed, placid matron giving of the fruits of her bounteous breasts to a male child. Then I knew that this was that same Goddess who stood over the outer door of the place, and was well pleased to find that the people, howsoever ignorantly, adored the power that enwombs the world,— Venus, the life-bringer and quickener of things that breathe,—and could, in this matter, touch hearts with the wise. So with this thought, that truly God was one and men divers, I came out of the temple well pleased, into the level light of the day's beam.

In the tavern doorway, under a bush of green ilex, we sat down in company to eat bread and peaches sopped in the wine of the country, and talked very briskly of all the things we had seen and heard. And soon into the current of our discourse was drawn a dark-faced youth, who had been observing us earnestly for some time from under his hanging brows, and who, growing mighty curious (as I find the way of them is), must know who and whence we were and of what belief and condition in the world. So when I had satisfied him, "Turn for turn," said I, "my honest friend: being strangers, as you have learned, we have seen many things which touch us nearly, and some which are hard of reading. But this very reading is to us of high concernment, for these matters relate to religion, and religion, of what sort soever it may be, no man can venture to despise. For certain I am, that, as a man hath never seen the gods, so he may never be sure that he hath ever conceived them, even darkly, as in a mirror. For we are dwellers in a cave, my friend, with our backs to the light, and may not tell of a truth whether the shadows that flit and fade be indeed gods or no. Tell me, therefore (for I am puzzled by it), is the goddess whose presentment I yet see over your temple-porch, that Mother of gods and men, yea, even Mother of life itself, to whom we also bend the neck ? "

PEACHES AND WINE

"She is, sir, as we believe, Mother of God; and therefore, God being author of life, Mother of life and all things living."

"It is as I had believed," said I, "and you, young sir, and I, may bow together in that temple of hers without offence. For the temple is to her honour as I conceive?"

"Why, yes," he answered, "it is raised to her most holy name and to that of our Lord."

"And your Lord, who is this? and which altar is his? For there are many."

"The great altar is his, and indeed he is to be worshipped in all," said the young man.

"He is then the tortured god, whose semblance hangs upon the black cross?"

"He is."

Then I begged him to tell me why these mournful images were scattered over his goodly earth, these maimed gods, this blood and weeping; but I may not set down all that he told me, seeing that much of it was dark, and much, as I thought, not pertinent to the issue. Much again was said with his hands, which I cannot interpret here. Suffice it that I learned this concerning the Agonist, that he was the son of the goddess and greater than she, though in a sense less. Mortal he was, and immortal, abject to look upon, being indeed accounted a malefactor and crucified like a thief; and yet a king of men, speaking wisdom whereof the like hath hardly been heard. For of two things he taught there would seem to be no bottom to them, so profound and unsearchable they are. And one of them was this,—"The kingdom is within you" (or some such words); and the other was, "Who will lose his life shall save it." Whereof, methinks, the first comprehends all the teaching of the Academy and the second that of the Porch. So this man must needs have been a god, and whether the son or no of the Soul of the World, greater than she. For what she did, as it were by necessity and her blind inhering power, he *knew*. Therefore he must have been Wisdom itself. And thus I knew that he could not be Dionysus the Saviour, though he might have many of his attributes; nor simply that son of Venus whom Ausonius alone of our poets saw fastened to a cross. So at last, "I will tell you," said I, "who this god really is, as it seems to me. Being of vile estate and yet greatest of all; being mortal and yet immortal, god and man; being at once most wise and most simple, and (as such his condition imports) intermediate between Earth and Heaven, he must needs be the Divine Eros, concerning whom Plato's words are yet with us. So I can understand why he is so wise, why he suffers always, and yet cannot be driven by torment nor persuaded by sophisms to cease loving. For the necessity of love is to crave ever; and he is Love himself. Wherefore I am very sure he can lead men, if they will, from the fair things of the world to those infinitely fairer things in themselves whereby what we now have are so very fair to see. And he may well be son of this goddess and nourished by her milk; for it behoves us that a god should stand between Earth and Heaven and be compact of the elements of either, so that he should condescend the wisdom of his head to instruct the clemency of his heart. And we know, you and I, that the gods are but attributes of God, whose intellect (as I say) may well be in Heaven, but his heart is in the Earth, and is the core of it. For so we say of the poet that his heart is ever in his fair work."

Thus we took our wine and were well content to sit in the sunshine.

IV

OF POETS AND NEEDLEWORK

THE man of our time to class poetry as a thing very pleasant and useful shall hardly be found. At most the saying will suffer reprint as a quaintness, a freak, or a paradox ; and so it has proved. From Prato, dusty little city of mid-Tuscany, and with the impress of its Reale Orfanotrofio (nourisher, it would thus appear, of more Humanities than one), comes an " *Opera Nova, nella quale si contengono bellissime historie, contrasti, lamenti e frottole, con alcune canzoni a ballo, strambotti, geloghe, farse, capitoli e bazellette di più eccellenti autori. Aggiuntevi assai tramutationi, villanelle alla napolitana, sonetti alla bergamasca e mariazi alla povana, indovinelli, ritoboli e passerotti* "; *cosa,* this legend goes on to say, *molto piacevole ed utile.* This is, no doubt, rococo, and at best a pitiful, catchfarthing bit of ancientry : yet it looks back to a time when it was indeed the fact that no choice work could be but useful, and when eyes and ears, as conduits to the soul, had that full of consideration we reserve for mouth and nose, purveyors to the belly.

Vasari, Giorgio, he too, *bourgeois* though he were, and in so far the best of testimony, knew it when he found Luca's blue and white to be "molto utile per la state." We should say that of a white umbrella or suit of flannels ; why of earthenware or an adroit *strambotto* ? That marks the cleft, the incurable gulf of difference, between a people like the Tuscans with art in their marrow, and our present selves with our touching reliance upon a most unseemly hunger after facts. I suppose I should be stretching a point if I said that *Samson Agonistes* was *cosa molto piacevole ed utile.* And yet I name there a great poem and a weighty, whence the general public suck, or claim to suck, no small advantage. Is it more useful to them than Bradshaw ? I doubt. But here, in this Opera Nova so furthered, are sixty-three little snatches of Luigi Pulci's, eight lines to the stave, about the idlest of make-believe love affairs, full of such Petrarchisms as "Gl' occhi tuoi belli son li crudel dardi," or

"Tu m'ai trafitto il cor ! donde io moro,
Se tu, iddea, non mi dai aiutoro,"—

the merest commonplaces of gallantry :
called on what account by their contrivers
molto utile ?

I have urged in my Second Essay that the
Tuscans were inveterate weavers of fancy,
choosing what came easiest to hand to
weave withal. I dared to see such airy
spinning in that Spanish Chapel from which
Mr. Ruskin has nearly frightened the lovers
of Art ; I said that the *Summa* was to the
painters there as good vantage-ground as
any novel of Sacchetti's. I now say that
Luigi Pulci and his kindred so treated the
love-lore which was solemn mystery to
Guinicelli and Lapo and Fazio, or the young
Dante shuddering before his lord of terrible
aspect. I would add Petrarch's name to
this honourable roll if I believed it fitting
such a niche ; but I find him the greatest
equivocator of them all, and owe him a
grudge for making a fifteenth-century Dante
impossible. It is true, had there been such
a poet we should never have had our Milton ; but that may not serve the Swan of
Vaucluse as justification for being miserable
before a looking-glass, that he starved his

grandsons to serve ours. Take him then
as a poser : give him, for the argument's
sake, Boccace to his company, Cino ; give
him our Pulci, give him Ariosto, give him
Lorenzo, Politian ; give him Tasso for aught
I care ; you have no one left but the sugar-
cured Guarino. Dante stands alone upon
the skyey peaks of his great argument,
steadied there and holding his breath, as
for the hush that precedes weighty endeav-
our ; and Bojardo (no Tuscan by birth)
stands squarely to the plains, holding out
one hand to Rabelais over-Alps and another
to Boccace grinning in his grave. The fellow is such a sturdy pagan we must e'en
forgive him some of his quirks. Italian
poesy, poor lady, stript to the smock, can
still look honestly out if she have but two
such vestments whole and unclouted as the
Commedia and the *Orlando*. Let us look
at some of her spoiled bravery. Take up
my Opera Nova and pick over Pulci in his
lightest mood. I am minded to try my
hand for your amusement.

" Let him rejoice who can ; for me, I 'd grieve.
Peace be with all ; for me yet shall be war.
Let him that hugs delight, hug on, and leave
To me sweet pain, lest day my night shall mar.

I am struck hard ; the world, you may believe,
Laughs out ;—rejoice, my world ! I 'll pet my scar.
Rogue love, that puttest me to such a pass,
They cry thee, ' It is well ! ' I sing, ' Alas ! ' "

Vers de société ? No ; too rhetorical :
your antithesis gives headaches to fine ladies. Euphuist ? Not in the applied sense :
read Shakespere's sonnets in that manner ;
or, if you object that Shakespere is too
high for such comparisons, read Drum-
mond of Hawthornden. Poetry, which has
a soul, we cannot call it. Verse it assuredly is, and of the most excellent. Just receive a quatrain of the pure spring and
judge for yourself :

" Chi gode goda, che pur io stento ;
Chi è in pace si sia, ch'io son in guerra ;
Chi ha diletto l'habbi, ch'io ho tormento ;
Chi vive lieto, in me dolor afferra."

Balance is there. Vocalisation, adjust-
ment of sound, discriminate use of long
syllables and short, of subjunctive and in-
dicative moods.* Unpremeditated art it is
not : indeed it is craft rather than art ; for

* More than that : the piece is an excellent example
of the skilful use of redundant syllables. It is certain
that a study of Italian poetry would help our, too often,
tame blank verse to be (however bad otherwise) at least

Art demands a larger share of soul-expenditure than Pulci could afford. And of such is the delicate ware which Tuscany, nothing doubting, took for *lavoro molto utile.* For, believe it or not, of that kind were Della Robbia's enrichments, Ghirlandajo's frescos, Raphael's Madonnas, and Alberti's broad marble churches : of that kind and of no other ; on a level with the painted lady smiling out of a painted window at Airolo, whose frozen lips assure the traverser of the Saint Gothard that he has passed the ridge and may soon smell the olives.

Wherein, then, is the use ? Why, it is in the art of it. I will convict you out of Alberti's own mouth, or his biographer's, for he spake it truly. "For he was wont to say," thus runs the passage, "that whatever might be accomplished by the wit of man with a certain choiceness, that indeed was next to the divine." To image the divine, you see, you must accomplish somewhat, scrupulously weigh, select, and refuse ; in short adapt exquisitely your means

not dull. It might bring it nearer to Milton, as Dante brought Keats. Witness his revision of *Hyperion.* If the Tuscans over-rated the craft in Poetry, we assuredly under-rate it.

5

until they are adequate to your ends. And, keeping the eye steadily on that, you might grow to discard solemn ends, or moment- ous, altogether, until poetry and painting ceased to be arts at all, and must be classed, at best, with needlework. So indeed it proved in the case of poetry. After Politian (who really did catch some echo of other times, and of manners more primal than his own, and did instil something of it in his *Orfeo*) no poet of Italy had anything seri- ous to say. I doubt it even of Tasso, though Tasso, I know, has a vogue. I ex- cept, of course, Michael Angelo, as I have already said ; and I except Boccace and Bojardo. Painting was drawn out of the pit laid privily for her by the sheer neces- sity of an outlet ; and painting, having much to say, became the representative Italian art. Poetry, the most ancient of them all, as she is the most majestic; the art which refuses to be taught, and alone of her sisters must be acquired by self- spenditure (so that before you can learn to string your words in music you must be shaken with a thought which, to your tor- turing, you must spoil); poetry, at once music and soothsay, knitted to us as touching her common speech, and to the spheres as touching on the same immortal harmonies ; poetry such as Dante's was, was gone from Tuscany, and painting, to her own ruining, reigned instead, drawing in sculpture and architecture to share her kingdom and attributes. Which indeed they did, to their equal detriment and our discouragement that read.

When I want to see Death in small-clothes bowing in the drawing-room I turn to my Petrarch and open at Sonnet cclxxxii. where it is written how :

" It lies with Death to take the beauty of Laura but not the gracious memory of her ";

As thus :

" Now hast thou touch'd thy stretch of power, O Death ;
Thy brigandage hath beggar'd Love's demesne
And quench'd the lamp that lit it, and the queen
Of all the flowers snapped with thy ragged teeth.
Hollow and meagre stares our life beneath
The querulous moon, robb'd of its sovereign :
Yet the report of her, her deathless mien—
Not thine, O churl ! Not thine, thou greedy Death !
They are with her in Heaven, the which her grace,
Like some brave light, gladdens exceedingly
And shoots chance beams to this our dwelling-place :
So art thou swallowed in her victory.
Yet on me, beauty-whelmed in very sooth,
On me that last-born angel shall have ruth."

Look in vain for the deep heart-cry that voiced Dante's passion in the tremendous statements of this :

" Beatrice is gone up into high Heaven,
  The kingdom where the angels are at peace ;
  And lives with them : and to her friends is dead.
  Not by the frost of winter was she driven
  Away, like others ; nor by summer heats ;
  But through a perfect gentleness, instead.
  For from the lamp of her meek lowlihead
  Such an exceeding glory went up hence
  That it woke wonder in the Eternal Sire,
  Until a sweet desire
  Entered Him for that lovely excellence,
  So that He bade her to Himself aspire ;
  Counting this weary and most evil place
  Unworthy of a thing so full of grace."
                                    (D. G. ROSSETTI.)

Now and again it may happen that a poet, ridden by the images of his thought, can " state the facts " and leave the rhyme to chance. The Greeks, to whom facts were rarer and of more significance, one supposes, than they are to us, did it habitually. That is what gives such irresistible import to Homer and to Sophocles. They knew that the adjective is the natural enemy of the verb. The naked act, the bare thought, a sequence of stately-balanced rhythm and that ensuring harmony of sentences, gave their poetry its distinction. They did not wilfully colour their verse, if they did, as I suppose we must admit, their statues. "Now," says Sir Thomas, "there is a musick wherever there is a harmony, order or proportion ; and thus far we may maintain the musick of the spheres; for those well-ordered motions, and regular paces, though they give no sound unto the ear, yet to the understanding they strike a note most full of harmony." After the Greeks, Dante, who may have drawn *lo bello stile* from Virgil, but hardly his great notes, as of a bell, carried on the tradition of directness and naked strength. But Petrarch, and after him all Tuscany, dallied with light thinking, and beat all the images of Love's treasury into thin conventions.

Però, what gentlemen they were, these "ingegni fiorentini," these Tuscan wits ! What innate breeding and reticence ! What punctilious loyalty to the little observances of literature, of wall-decoration, call it, in the most licentiously-minded of them ! Lorenzo Magnifico was a rake and could write lewdly enough, as we all know. Yet, when he chose, that is, when Art bade

him, how unerringly he chose the right
momentum. His too was "la mente che
non erra." I found this of his the other
day, and must needs close up my notes
with it. The very notion of it was, in his
time, a convention ; a series of sonnets
bound together by an argument ; a *Vita
nova* without its overmastering occasion.
Simonetta was dead ; whereupon "tutti i
fiorentini ingegni, come si conviene in sì
pubblica jattura, diversamente ed avversa-
mente si dolsono, chi in versi, chi in prosa."
The poor dead lady was, in fact, a butt for
these sharpshooters. Yet hear Lorenzo.

"Died, as we have declared, in our city a certain
lady, whereby all people alike in Florence were moved
to compassion. And this is no marvel, seeing that with
all earthly beauty and courtesy she was adorned as,
before her day, no other under heaven could have been.
Among her other excellent parts, she had a carriage so
sweet and winsome that whosoever should have any
commerce or friendly dealing with her, straightway fell
to believe himself enamoured of her. Ladies also, and
all youth of her degree, not only suffered no harbourage
to unkindly thought upon this her eminence over all the
rest, nor grudged it her at all, but stoutly upheld and
took pleasure in her loveliness and gracious bearing ; and
this so honestly that you would have found it hard to be
believed so many men without jealousy could have
loved her, or so many ladies without envy give her

place. So, the more her life by its comely ordering had endeared her to mankind, pity also for her death, for the flower of her youth, and for a beauteousness which in death, it may be, showed the more resplendently than in life, did breed in the heart the smarting of great desire. Therefore she was carried uncovered on the bier from her dwelling to the place of burial, and moved all men, thronging there to see her, to abundant shedding of tears. And in some, who before had not been aware of her, after pity grew great marvel for that she, in death, had overcome that loveliness which had seemed insuperable while she yet lived. Among which people, who before had not known her, there grew a bitterness and, as it were, ground of reproach, that they had not been acquainted with so fair a thing before that hour when they must be shut off from it for ever ; to know her thus and have perpetual grief of her. But truly in her was made manifest that which our Petrarch had spoken when he said,

' Death showed him lovely in her lovely face.' "

This is to write like a gentleman and an artist, with ear attuned to the subtlest fall and cadence, with scrupulous weighing of words that their true outline shall hold clear and sharp. It is *intarsiatura*, skilful and clean at the edges. He goes on to play with his hammered thought, always as delicately and precisely as before.

" Falling, therefore, such an one to death, all the wits of Florence, as is seemly in so public a calamity,

71

lamented severally and mutually, some in rhyme, some
in prose, the ruefulness of it ; and bound themselves
to exalt her excellence each after the contriving of his
mind : in which company I, too, must needs be ; I,
too, mingle rhymes with tears. So I did in the sonnets
below rehearsed ; whereof the first began thus :

    ' O limpid shining star, that to thy beam.'

  " Night had fallen : together we walked, a dear
friend and I, together talking of our common sorrow :
and so speaking, the night being wondrous clear, I
lifted my eyes to a star of exceeding brilliancy, which
appeared in the West, of such assured splendour as not
alone to excel other stars, but so eagerly to shine that it
threw in shadow all the lights of heaven about it.
Whereof having great marvel, I turned to my friend,
saying : ' We ought not to wonder at this sight, seeing
that the soul of that most gentle lady is of a truth either
re-informed in this, a new star, or conjoined to shine
with it. Wherefore there is no marvel in such exceeding
brightness ; and we who took comfort in her living
delights, may even now be appeased by her appearance
in a limpid star. And if our vision for such a light
is tender and fragile, we should beseech her shade, that
is the god in her, to make us bolder by withholding
some part of her beam that we may sometimes look
upon her, nor sear our eyes. But, to say sooth, this is
no overboldness in her, endowed as she was with all the
power of her beauty, that she should strive to shine
more excellently than all the other stars, or even yet more
proudly with Phœbus himself, asking of him his very
chariot, that she, rather, may rule our day. Which
thing, if you allow it without presumption in our star,

how vilely shows the impertinence of Death to have laid hands upon such loveliness and authority as hers.' And since these my reasonings seemed of the stuff proper for a sonnet, I took leave of my friend and composed that one which follows ; speaking in it of the above mentioned star."

The sonnet is in the right Petrarchian vein, adroit and shallow as you please. With such a preface it could hardly be otherwise — the invocation of the lady's shade, the twitting of Death (making his Mastership jig to suit their occasions who had of late been in his presence) and the naïve acceptance of all gifts as "buona materia a un sonetto."   In the end he spins four to her memory; then finds another lady and doubles all his superlatives for her. For the star, he remembers, may have been Lucifer ; and Lucifer is but herald of the day.   To it then ! with all the *buona materia a un sonetto* the dawn can give you. Thus flourished poetry in the Tuscan *quattrocentro ;* for Politian was but little more poet than Lorenzo, while he was no less dextrous as a rhymer and fashioner of conceits.   Not serious, but *piacevole,* with an *elegantia quædam prope divinum ;* therefore *molto utile.*   Pen-work in fact, and

73

kin to needlework. Because Tuscany saw choicely - wrought things pleasing, and pleasant things useful, we of to-day can see Florence as an open-air Museum. But we wrap our own Poets in heavy bindings and let them lie on drawing-room tables in company of *Whitaker's Almanac* and an album of photographs. Well, well! We must teach them to say, *Philistia, be thou glad of me,* I suppose.

V

OF BOILS AND THE IDEAL *

(A Colloquy with Perugino)

"THERE," said my Roman escort, as we forded the Tiber near Torgiano, "the haze is lifting : behold august Perugia." I looked out over the misty plain, and saw the spiked ridge of a hill, serried with towers and belfries as a port with ships' masts; then the grey stone walls and escarpments warm in the sun ; finally a mouth to the city, which seemed to engulph both the white road and the citizens walking to and fro upon it like flies. But it was some time yet before I could decipher the image on the gonfalon streaming in the breeze above the Signiory. It was actually, on a field vert, a griffin rampant sable, langued gules. "So ho !" said the guide when I had described it,

---

* This appeared in the *New Review* for December, 1896, and is reproduced by leave of the Publisher.

"So ho! the Mountain Cat is at home
again. . . . And here comes scouring one
of the whelps," he added in alarm. A
young man, black-avised, bare-headed,
pressing a lathered horse, bore down upon
us. He seemed to gain exultation with
every new pulse of his strength: the
Genius of Brute Force, handsome as he
was evil. And yet not evil, unless a wild
beast is evil; which it probably is not. He
soon reached us, pulled up short with a
clatter of hoofs, and hailed me in a raw
dialect, asking what I did, whence and who
I was, whither I went, what I would? As
he spake—looking at me with fierce eyes
in which pride, suspicion, and the shyness
of youth struggled and rent each other—he
fooled with a straight sword, and seemed
to put his demands rather to provoke a
quarrel than to get an answer. I wished
no quarrel with a boy, so, as my custom is,
I answered deliberately that I travelled, and
from Rome; that my name was Hewlett,
at his service; that I was going to Perugia;
that I would be rid of him. I saw him
grow loutish before my adroit impassivity;
his fencing was not with such tools. He
sulked, and must know next what I wanted

76

at Perugia. I told him I had business with
Pietro Vannucci, called Il Perugino by those
who admired him from a distance; and he
seemed relieved, withal a something of con-
tempt for my person fluttered on his pretty
lip. At any rate, he left fingering his steel
toy. "Peter the Pious!" he scoffed.
"Are you of his litter? Pots and Pans?
Off with you; you'll find him hoarding his
money or his wife. To the wife you may
send these from Semonetto. Whereat my
young gentleman fell to kissing his hand in
the air. I rose in my stirrups and bowed
elaborately, and, taking off my hat in the
act, put him to some shame, for he was
without that equipment. He pulled a wry
face at me, like any schoolboy, and can-
tered off on his spent horse, arms akimbo,
and his irons rattling about him. My guide
marked a furtive cross on his breast and
vowed, I am pretty sure, a score candles to
Santa Maria in Cosmedin if ever he reached
home. "God is good," he said, "God is
very good. That was Simon Baglione."

"He seemed a very unlicked cub," was
all my reply. So we climbed the dusty
steep, winding twice or thrice round about
the hill in a brown plain set with stubbed

77

trees, and entered the armed city by the
Porta Eburnea. Inside the walls, thread-
ing our way up a spiral lane among bullock-
carts, cloaked cavaliers, monks, fair-haired
girls carrying pitchers and baskets, bullies,
bravoes, and well - to - do burgesses, we
passed from one ambush to another, by
dark gullies, stinking traps, and twisted
stairways, to the Via Deliziosa, without
ever a hint of the broad sunshine or whiff
of the balmy air which we had left outside
on the plain.

In a little mildewed court, where one
patch of light did indeed slope upon a
lemon-tree loaded with fruit and flowers,
I found my man in a droll pass with his
young wife. He was, in fact, tiring her
hair in the open : nothing more ; nevertheless, there was that air of mystery in
the performance which made me at once
squeamish of going farther, and afraid to
withdraw. I stood, therefore, in confusion
while the sport went on. It was of his
seeking I could see, for the poor girl looked
shamefaced and weary enough. She was
a winsome child (no more), broad in the
brows, full in the eye, yellow-haired, like
most of the women in this place, with a

fine-shaped mouth, rather voluptuously underlipped ; and, as I then saw her, sitting in a carven chair with her hands at a listless droop over the arms of it. Her hair, which was loose about her and of great length and softness, lay at the mercy of her master. He, a short, pursy man, well over middle age—" past the Grand Climacteric," as Bulwer Lytton used to say—red and anxiously lined, stood behind her, barber fashion, and ran her hair through his fingers, all the while talking to himself very fast. His eyes were half-shut : he seemed ravished by the sight of so much gold (if common reports belie him not) or the feel of so much silk (the likelier opinion), I know not which. Assuredly so odd a beginning to my adventure, a hardier man would have stumbled !

The sport went on. The girl, as I considered her, was of slight, almost mean figure ; her good looks, which as yet lay rather in promise, resolved themselves into a small compass, for they ended at her shoulders. Below them she was slender to stooping, and with no shape to speak of. Allow her a fine little head, the timid freshness natural to her age, a blush-rose

skin, slim neck, and that glorious weight
of hair : there is Perugino's wife ! Add
that she was vested in a milky green robe
which was cut square and low at the neck
and fitted her close, and I have no more to
say on her score than she had on any. As for
the Maestro himself, I got to know him
better. On mere sight I could guess something of him. A master evidently, unhappy
when not ordering something ; fidgety by
the same token ; yet a fellow of humours,
and fertile of inventions whereon to feed
them. The more I considered him the
more subtle ministry to his pleasures did
I find this morning's work to be. A man,
finally, happiest in dreams. I looked at
him now in that vein. In and out, elbow-
deep sometimes, went his hands and arms,
plunging, swimming in that luxurious
mesh of hair. He sprayed it out in a
shower for Danaë ; he clutched it hard and
drew it into thick burnished ropes of fine
gold. Anon, as the whim caught him,
he would pile it up and hedge it with
great silver pins, fanshape, such as country girls use, till it took the semblance,
now of a tower, now of a wheel, now of
some winged beast—sphinx or basilisk—

couching on the girl's head. Then, stepping
back a little, he would clasp his hands over
his eyes, and with head in air sing some
snatch of triumph, or laugh aloud for the
very wildness of his power; and so the
game went on, that seemed a feast of
delight to the man—a feast? an orgie of
sense. But the woman might have been
cut in stone. Had she not breathed, or
had not her fingers faintly stirred now and
again, you would have sworn her a wax
doll.

I know not how long the two might have
stayed at their affairs, for here I grew
wearied and, coughing discreetly, slid my
foot on the flags. The man looked up,
stopped his play at once; the spell was
broken. The girl, I noticed, stirred not at
all, but sat on as she was, with her hair about
her clasping her shoulders and flooding her
with gold. But Master Peter was a little
disconcerted, I am pretty sure; certainly he
was redder than usual about the gills and
gullet. He cleared his throat once or twice
with an attempt at pomposity which he
vainly tried to sustain as he came out to
meet me. When I handed him the Pro-
thonotary's letter, and he saw the broad

6

seal, he bowed quite low; the letter read, he took me by the hand and led me to the loggia of his house. We had to pass Madam on the way thither; but by this Master Peter carried off the affair as coolly as you choose. "Imola, child," he said as we passed, "I have company. Put up thy hair and fetch me out a fiaschone of Orvieto —that of the year before last. Be sure thou makest no mistake; and break no bottles, girl, for the wine is good. And hard enough to come by," he added with a sigh. The girl obeyed. Without raising her eyes she rose; without raising them she put her hands to her head and deftly braided and coiled her hair into a single twist; still looking down to earth she passed into the house.

Pietro began to talk briskly enough so soon as we were set. The air was mild for mid-March; between the ridged tiles of the cortile, which ran up to a great height, I could see a square of pale blue sky; gnats were busy in the beam of dusty light which slanted across the shade; I heard the bees about the lemon-bush droning of a quiet and opulent summer hovering nearby. It was a very peaceful and well-disposed world just then. Pietro, much at his ease, was apt to take life as he found it—nor do I wonder.

"Yes," he said, "the work goes; the work goes. I have much to do; you may call me just now quite a man of affairs. This very morning, now, I received a little deputation from Città di Castello—quite a company! The Prior, the Sub-Prior, two Vicars-Choral, two Wardens of Guilds, and other gentlemen, craving a piece by my own hand for the altar of Saint Roch. I thank our Lord I can pick and choose in these days. I told them I would think of it, whereat they seemed to know relief, but I added, How did they wish the boil treated, on the Saint's left thigh? For I told them, and I was very firm, that though Holy Church might aver the boil to have been a grievous boil, a boil indeed, yet my art could have little to say to boils, as boils. The boil must be a great boil, and a red, said they; for the populace love best what they know best, and cannot worship, as you might say, with maimed rites. Moreover, Poggibonsi had a Saint Roch done by that luxurious Sienese Bazzi (a man of scandalous living, as I daresay you know), where the boil was fiery to behold and as big as a man's ankle-bone. This was a cause of new great devotion among the impious by reason of its plain relationship to our frail flesh. Città was a poor city; in fine, there must be a handsome boil. I said, Let me refine upon the boil, and Saint Roch is yours, with Madonna, in addition, caught up in clouds of pure light, and two fiddling angels, one at either hand. Finally, with the petition that Madonna should be rarely adorned with pearls Flemish-fashion, they let me have my way upon the boil. So the work goes on ! "

" But, good Master Peter," I exclaimed here, " I could find some discrepancy in this. On the one hand you boggle at boils, on the other you suffer pearls to be thrust upon you. Why, if you cleave to the one, should you despise the other? For, for aught I see, your thesis should exclude either."

" And so it does," he said, smiling. "But for one man in Città that knows a pearl there will be a hundred who can judge of a boil. My Madonna will be a pearl-faced Umbrian maid, and her other pearls just as Flemish as I choose. But I hear our glasses clinking."

I, too, heard Imola's footfall on the flags,

and ventured to say, "And I know where your Madonna is, Master Peter." But he affected not to hear.

She served us our amber cup with the same persistent, almost sullen, self-continence. But, I thought, I must see your eyes, Mistress, for once; so called to mind my encounter with the wild young Baglione of the morning. Smiling as easily as I could, I accosted her with "Madonna, I am the bearer of compliments to you, if you choose to hear them." Then she looked me full for a second of time. I saw by her dilating eyes, wide as a hare's (though of a sea-grey colour), that she was not always queen of herself, and pitied her. For it is ill to think of broken-in hearts, or souls set in bars, and I could fancy Master Peter's hand not so light upon her as upon church-walls. But I went on, "Yes, Madonna, even as I rode up hither, I met a young knight-at-arms who wished you as well as you were fair, and kissed your hands as best he might, considering the distance, before he rode off." Imola blushed, but said nothing.

"Who was this youth, sir?" asked Master Peter, in a hurry.

"It was plainly some young noble of your State," said I, "but for his name I know nothing, for he told me nothing." I added this quickly, because I could see our friend was keen enough for all his coat of unconcern, and I feared the whip by and by for Imola's thin shoulders. But I knew quite well who the boy was. Imola went lightly away without any sign of twitter. I turned to Master Peter again.

"In this matter of boils and pearls," I began, "I would not deny but you are in the right, and yet there is this to be said. The Greeks of whose painting, truly, we have next to nothing, in all the work of theirs known to us did what lay before them as well as ever they could. They stayed not to theorise over this axiom and that, that formula and this. They said rather, You wish for the presentment of a man with a boil on his leg? Well. And they produced both man and boil."

"Why yes, yes," broke in my friend, "that is plain enough. But apart from this, that you are talking of sculpture to me who do but paint, you should know very well that your Greek copied no single boil, no, nor no probable boil, but, as it were, the summary and perfect conclusion of all possible boils."

" *To Pithanon ?* Yes; I admit it. For Aristotle says as much."

"Right so do I, in my degree and by my art," said Perugino; "and without knowing anything of Aristotle save that he was wise."

"Your pardon, my brave Vannucci," I said, "but you have admitted the opposite of this. Did you not hint to the deputation that you would give Saint Roch no boils ? And have you ever let creep into your pieces the semblance of so much as a pimple ? Remember, I know your *Sebastian ;* and know, also, Il Sodoma's, which he made as a banner for the Confraternity of that famous Saint in Camollia."

" I seek the essence of fact," he replied, " which, believe me, never lay in the displacement of an arrow-point: no, nor in the head of a boil. Bazzi is a sensualist : as his palate grows stale he whets it by stronger meat; thinks to provoke appetite by disgust; would draw you on by a nasty inference, as a dog by his hankering after fæcal odours. What nearness to Art in his plumpy boy stuck with arrows like a skewered capon? Causes nuns to weep, hey? and to dream dreams, hey? Nature would do that cleanlier; and waxwork more powerfully! Form, my good sir, Form is your safeguard. Lay hold on Form; you are as near to Essence as may be here below. Art works for the rational enlargement of the fancy, not the titillation of sense. And Invention is the more sacred the closer it apes the scope of the divine plan. And this much, at least, of the Grecian work I have learned, that it will never lick vulgar shoes, nor fawn to beastly eyes. It is a stately order, a high pageant, a solemn gradual, wherein the beholder will behold just so much as he is prepared, by litany and fasting and long vigil, to receive. No more and no less."

" Aristotle again," said I, "with his ' continual slight novelty.' No fits and starts."

"I have told you before I know nothing of the man," said Perugino, vexed, it appeared, at such wounding of his vanity to be new; " let me tell you this. There are fellows abroad who dub me dunce and dull - head. The young Buonarroti, forsooth, who mistakes the large for the great, quantity for quality ; who in the indetermined pretends to see the mysterious. Mystery, quotha ! Mystery may be in an astrologer's horoscope, in a diagram. Mystery needs no puckered virago, nor bully in the sulks. There is mystery in the morning calms, mystery in a girl's melting mood; mystery in the irresolution of a growing boy full of dreams. But behold! it is there, not here. If you see it not, the fault is your own. It may be broad as day, cut clean as with a knife, displayed at large before a brawling world too busy lapping or grudging to heed it. The many shall pass it by as they run huddling to the dark. Yet the few shall adore therein the excellency of the mystery, even as the few (the very few) may discern in the flake of wafer-bread the shining wholeness of the Divine Nature——"

" 'The few remain, the many change and pass,' " I interpolated in a murmur. But Perugino never heeded me. He went on :

"The Greek, young sir, took the fact and let it alone to breed. His act lay in the taking and setting. Just so much import as it had borne it bore still; just so much weight as separation from its fellows lent

it was to his credit who first cut it free.
But nowadays glamour suits only with
serried muscles, frowns, and writhen lips ;
where darkness is we shudder, saying,
Behold a great mystery! Let a painter de-
clare his incompetence to utter, it shall be
enough to assure you he has walked with
God; for if he stammers, look you, that
testifies he is overwhelmed. Amen, I
would answer. Let his head swim and be
welcome; but let him not set to painting
till he can stand straight again. For in one
thing I am no Greek, in that I cannot hold
drunkenness divine." Here the good man
stopped for want of breath and I whipped in.

"Your great *Crucifixion* in Santa Maria
Maddalena," I began.

"Look you, sir," he took me up, "I
know what you would be at. Take that
piece (which is of my very best) or another
equally good, I mean the *Charge to Peter*
in Pope Sixtus his new Chapel, and listen
to me. The first thing your painter must
seek to do is to fill his wall. Let there be
no mistake about this. He is at first no
prophet nor man of God ; he is no jug-
gler nor mountebank who shall be re-
warded according to the enormity of his

grins ; his calling, maybe, is humbler, for all he stands for is to wash a wall so that no eye be set smarting because of it. Now that seems a very simple matter ; it is just as simple as the eye itself—so you may judge the validity of the arguments against me, that a wholesome green or goodly red wash would suffice. It would suffice indifferent well for a kennel of dogs. But mark this. Although your painter may drop hints for the soul, let him not strain above his pitch lest he crack his larynx. To his colour he may add form in the flat ; but he cannot escape the flat, however he may wriggle, any more than the sculptor can escape the round, scrape he never so wisely. Buonarroti will scrape and shift ; the Fleming has scraped and shifted all his days to as little purpose. His seed-pearls invite your touch. Touch them, my friend, you will smear your fingers. *Ne sutor ultra crepidam.* Leave miracles, O painter, to the Saint, and stick to your brush-work. Colour and form in the flat ; there is his armour to win the citadel of a man's soul."

" They call you mawkish," I dared to say.

"I am in good company," said the little man, with much pomposity.

"You say boldly, then, if I catch the chain of your argument"—thus I pursued him—"that you present (as by some formula which you have elaborated) the facts of religion in colour and design? For I suppose you will allow that your Art is concerned at least as much with religion as with the washing of walls?"

"Religion! Religion!" cried he. "What are you at? Concerned with religion! Man alive, it is concerned with itself; it *is* religion. I see you are very far indeed from the truth, and as you have spoken of my *Crucifixion* in Florence, now you shall suffer me to speak of it. I testify what I know, not that which I have not seen. And as mine eyes have never filled with blood from Golgotha, so I do not conjure with tools I have not learned to handle. But I will tell you what I have seen. The Mass: whereof my piece is, as it were, the transfiguration or a parable. For it grew out of a Mass I once heard, stately-ordered, solemnly and punctiliously served in a great church. Mayhap, I dreamed of it; we shall not quarrel over terms. It was a strange Mass, shorn of much ornament and circumstance, I thought, as I knelt and wondered : Here are no lamentations, no bruisèd breasts, no out-poured hearts, nor souls on flames. The day for tears is past, the fires are red, not flaming ; this is a day for steadfast regard, for service, patience, and good hope ; this is a day for Art to chant what the soul hath endured. For Art is a fruit sown in action and watered to utterance by tears. Two priests only, clothed in fine linen, served the Mass : ornaments of candles, incense, prostration, genuflection, there were none. Yet, step by step, and with every stop pondered reverently ere another was laid to its fellow's foundation ; with full knowledge of the end ere yet was the beginning accomplished ; in every gesture, every pause, intonation, invocation, stave of song, phrase of prayer ; by painful de-grees wrought in the soul's sweat and tears, unadorned, cold as fine stone, yet glittering none the less like fair marble set in the sun—was that solemn Mass sung through in the bare Church to the glory of God and His angels, who must ever rejoice in a work done so that the master-mind is straining and on watch over heart and voice. And I said, Calvary is done and the woe of it turned to triumph. Love is the fulfilling of the Law. Henceforth, for me Law shall be the fulfilment of my Love.

"Therefore I paint no terrors of death, no flesh torn by iron, no passion of an anguish greater than we can ever conceive, no bitter-sweet ecstasy of Self abandoned or Love inflaming ; but instead, serenity, a morning sky, a meek victim, Love fulfilling Law. Shorn of accidents, for the essence is enough ; not passionate, for that were as gross an affront in face of such awful death as to be trivial. Nothing too much ; Law fulfilling Love ; reasonable service.

"And because we are of the earth earthy, and because what I work you must behold with bodily eyes, I limn you angels and gods in your own image ; not of greater stature nor of more excellent beauty than many among you ; not of finer essence, maybe, than yourselves. But as the priests about that naked altar, so stand they, that the love which transfigures them be absorbed in the fulfilling of law ; and the law they exquisitely follow be at once the pattern and glass of their love."

Master Peter drained a beaker of his Orvieto. I admired; for indeed the little man spoke well.

"Now the Lord be good to you, Master Peter," I said; "men do you a great wrong. For there are some who aver that you doubt."

"Who does not doubt?" replied my host. "We doubt whenever we cannot see."

"I believe you are right," said I. "Your great Saint is, after all, your great Seer. For you, then, to question the soul's immortality is but to admit that you do not yet see your own life to come."

"Leave it so," said Perugino. "Let us talk reasonably."

"Did all men love the law as you do," I resumed after a painful pause—for I felt the force of the Master's rebuke to my impertinence (and could hope others will feel it also)—"did all love the law as you do, the world would be a cooler place and passion at a discount. But I cannot conceive Art without passion."

"Nor I," said the painter, "and for the excellent reason that there is no such thing. But remember this: passion is like the Alpheus.

95

Hedge it about with dams, you drive it deeper. Out of sight is not out of being. And the issue must needs be the fairer."

"Happy the passion," I said, "which hath an issue. There is passion of the vexed sort, where the tears are frozen to ice as they start. Of the tortured thus, remember—

'Lo pianto stesso lì pianger non lascia,
    E il duol, che trova in su gli occhi rintoppo,
    Si volve in entro a far crescer l'ambascia.' "

"You know our Dante ?" said Master Peter blandly (though I swear he knew what I was at). "There may be such people ; doubtless there are such people. For me, I find a perpetual outlet in my art." I could not forbear :

"Master Peter, Master Peter," I cried out, "how can I believe you when I know that your Madonna's eyes are brimming ; when I know why she turns them to a misty heaven or an earth seen blotted by reason of tears ? Do these tears ever fall, Master Peter ? or who freezes them as they start ?"

For I wondered where his patient Imola found her outlet, and whether young Simone has shown her a way. Master Peter drummed on the table and nursed one fat leg.

Before I took leave of the urbane little painter, in fact while I stood in the act of handshaking, I saw her white face at an upper window, looming behind rigid bars. On a sudden impulse I concluded my farewells rapidly and made to go. Vannucci turned back into the house and closed the door ; but I stayed in the cortile pretending a trouble with my spurs. Sure enough, in a short time I heard a light footfall. Imola stood beside me.

"Wish me a safe journey," I said smiling, "and no more bare-headed cavaliers on the road." Her lips hardly moved, so still her voice was. "Was he bareheaded ?" she asked, as if in awe.

"Love-locks floating free," I answered her gaily enough. "Shall I thank him for his courtesies to you, Madonna, if we meet ?"

"You will not meet : he is gone to Spello," she began, and then stopped, blushing painfully.

"But I may stay in Spello this night and could seek him out."

She was mistress of her lips, and could now look steadily at me. "I wish him very well," said Imola.

VI

THE SOUL OF A FACT

IN the days when it was verging on a
question whether a man could be at
the same time a good Christian and an
artist, the chosen subjects of painting were
significant of the approaching crisis—those
glaring moral contrasts in history which,
for want of a happier term, we call dramatic. Why this was so, whether Art took
a hint from Politics, or had withdrawn her
more intimate manifestations to await likelier times, is a question it were long to
answer. The subjects, at any rate, were
such as the Greeks, with their surer instincts and saving grace of sanity in matters
of this kind, either forbore to meddle with
or treated as decoratively as they treated
acanthus-wreaths. To-day we call them
" effective" subjects ; we find they produce shocks and tremors ; we think it
braces us to shudder, and we think that
Art is a kind of emotional pill ; we meas-
ure it quantitatively, and say that we

"know what we like." And doubtless there is something piquant in the quivering produced, for example, by the sight of white innocence fluttering helpless in a grey shadow of lust. So long as the Bible remained a god, that piquancy was found in a *Massacre of the Innocents;* in our own time we find it in a *Faust and Gretchen,* in the Doré Gallery, or in the Royal Academy. It was a like appreciation of the certain effect of vivid contrasts as powerful didactic agents (coupled with, or drowning, a something purer and more devout) which had inspired those most beautiful and distinctive of all the symbols of Catholicism, the *Adoration of the Kings,* the Christ-child cycle, and which raised the Holy Child and Maid-Mother to their place above the mystic tapers and the Cross. Naturally the Old Testament, that garner of grim tales, proved a rich mine: *David and Golias, Susanna and the Elders,* the *Sacrifice of Isaac, Jephthah's daughter.* But the story of Judith did not come to be painted in Tuscan sanctuaries until Donatello of Florence had first cast her in bronze at the prayer of Cosimo *pater patriæ.* Her entry was dramatic enough at least : Dame Fortune may well have sniggered as she spun round the city on her ball. Cosimo the patriot and his splendid grandson were no sooner dead and their brood sent flying, than Donatello's *Judith* was set up in the Piazza as a fit emblem of rescue from tyranny, with the vigorous motto, to make assurance double, "EXEMPLVM SALVTIS PVBLICÆ CIVES POSVERE." Savonarola, who knew his Bible, saw here a keener application of Judith's pious sin. A few years later that same *Judith* saw him burn. Thus, as an incarnate cynicism, she will pass ; as a work of art she is admittedly one of her great creator's failures. Her neighbour *Perseus* of the Loggia makes this only too plain ! For Cellini has seized the right moment in a deed of horror, and Donatello, with all his downrightness and grip of the fact, has hit upon the wrong. It is fatal to freeze a moment of time into an eternity of waiting. His *Judith* will never strike : her arm is palsied where it swings. The Damoclean sword is a fine incident for poetry ; but Holofernes was no Damocles, and, if he had been, it were intolerable to cast his experience in bronze. Donatello has essayed that thing impossible for sculpture, to arrest a

moment instead of denote a permanent at-
tribute. Art is adjectival, is it not, O Donatello ? Her business is to qualify facts, to
say what things are, not to state them, to
affirm that they are. A sculptured *Judith*
was done not long afterwards, carved, as
we shall see, with a burin on a plate ;
and the man who so carved her was a
painter.

Meantime, *pari passu,* almost, a painter
who was a poet was trying his hand ; a
man who knew his Bible and his mythology
and was equally at home with either. Perhaps it is not extravagant to say that you
cannot be an artist unless you are at home
with mythology, unless mythology is the
swiftest and most direct expression of your
being, so that you can be measured by it
as a man is known by his books, or a
woman by her clothes, her way of bowing,
her amusements, or her charities. For
mythopœia is just this, the incarnating the
spirit of natural fact ; and the generic name
of that power is Art. A kind of creation,
a clothing of essence in matter, an hypos-
tatising (if you will have it) of an object of
intuition within the folds of an object of
sense. Lessing did not dig so deep as his

Greek Voltaire (whose "dazzling antithesis," after all, touches the root of the matter),
for he did not see that rhythmic extension
in time or space, as the case may be, with
all that that implies—colour, value, proportion, all the convincing incidents of form—
is simply the mode of all arts, the thing
with which Art's substance must be inter-
penetrated, until the two form a whole,
lovely, golden, irresistible, and inevitable as
Nature's pieces are. This substance, I have
said, is the spirit of natural fact. And so
mythology is Art at its simplest and barest
(where the bodily medium is neither word,
nor texture of stone, nor dye), the parent
art from which all the others were, so to
speak, begotten by man's need. Thus
much of explanation, I am sorry to say, is
necessary, before we turn to our mytho-
poet of Florence, to see what he made out
of the story of Judith.

First of all, though, what has the story
of Judith to do with mythology ? It is a
legend, one of the finest of Semitic legends;
and between legend and myth there is as
great a gulf as between Jew and Greek. I
believe there are no myths proper to Israel
—I do not see how such magnificent

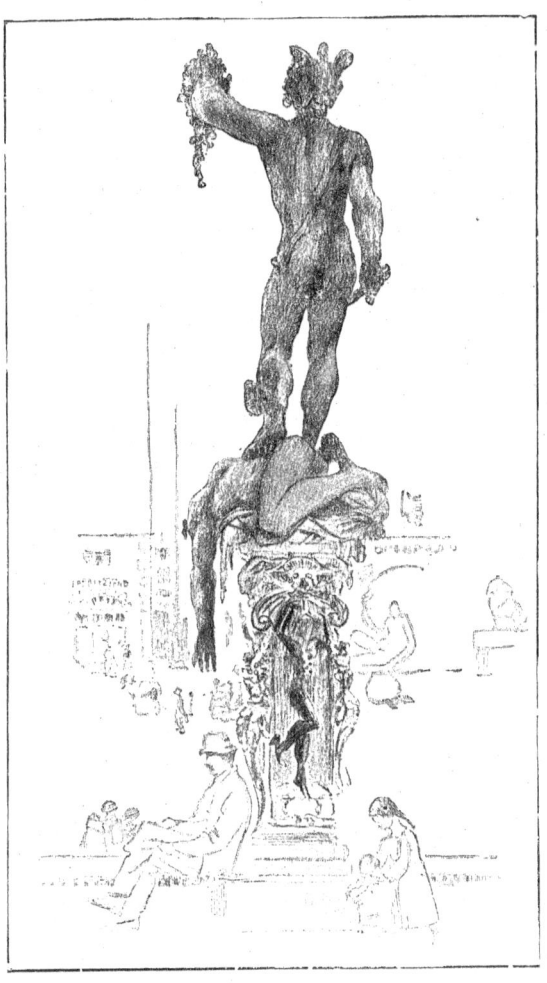

THE PERSEUS OF THE LOGGIA

egoists could contract to the necessary state
of awe—and I do not know that there are any
legends proper to Greece which are divorced
from real myths. For where a myth is the
incarnation of the spirit of natural fact, a
legend is the embellishment of an historical
event : a very different thing. A natural
fact is permanent and elemental, an historical event is transient and superficial. Take
one instance out of a score. The rainbow
links heaven and earth. Iris then, to the
myth-making Greek, was Jove's messenger,
intermediary between God and Man. That
is to incarnate a constant, natural fact.
Plato afterwards, making her daughter of
Thaumas, incarnated a fact, psychological,
but none the less constant, none the less
natural. But to say, as the legend-loving
Jew said, that Noah floated his ark over a
drowning world and secured for his poster-
ity a standing covenant with God, who
then and once for all set his bow in the
heavens ; that is to indicate, somewhere,
in the dim backward and abysm of time,
an historical event. The rainbow is
suffered as the skirt of the robe of Noah,
who was an ancestor of Israel. So the
Judith poem may be a decorated event, or

it may be the barest history in a splendid epical setting : the point to remember is that it cannot be, as a legend, a subject for creative art. The artist, in the language of Neo-Platonism, is a demiurge ; he only of men can convert dead things into life. And now we will go into the Uffizi.

Mr. Ruskin, in his petulant-playful way, has touched upon the feeling of amaze most people have who look for the first time at Botticelli's *Judith* tripping smoothly and lightly over the hill-country, her stead-fast maid dogging with intent, patient eyes every step she takes. You say it is flippant, affected, pedantic. For answer, I refer you to the sage himself, who, from his point of view—that painting may fairly deal with a chapter of history—is perfectly right. The prevailing strain of the story is the strength of weakness—*ex dulci fortitudo*, to invert the old enigma. " O God, O my God, hear me also, a widow. Break down their stateliness by the hand of a woman ! " It is the refrain that runs through the whole history of Israel, that reasonable compla-cency of a little people in their God-fraught destiny. And, withal, a streak of savage spite: that the audacious oppressor shall be

done scornfully to death. There is the
motive of Jael and Sisera too. So "she
smote twice upon his neck with all her
might, and she took away his head from
him, and tumbled his body down from the
bed." Ho ! what a fate for the emissary
of the Great King. Wherefore, once more,
the jubilant paradox, " The Lord hath smitten him by the hand of a woman ! " That
is it: the amazing, thrilling antithesis insisted on over and over again by the old
Hebrew bard. " Her sandals ravished his
eyes, her beauty took his mind prisoner,
and the fauchion passed through his neck."
That is the *leit-motif:* Sandro the poet
knew it perfectly well and taught it, to the
no small comfort of Mr. Ruskin and his
men. Giuditta, dainty, blue-eyed, a girl
still and three years a widow, flits home-
ward through a spring landscape of grey
and green and the smile of a milky sky,
being herself the dominant of the chord,
with her bough of slipt olive and her jagged
scimitar, with her pretty blue fal-lals
smocked and puffed, and her yellow curls
floating over her shoulders. On her slim
feet are the sandals that ravished his eyes ;
all her maiden bravery is dancing and

fluttering like harebells in the wind. Behind her plods the slave-girl folded in an
orange scarf, bearing that shapeless, nameless burden of hers, the head of the grim Lord
Holofernes. Oh, for that, it is the legend
itself ! For look at the girl's eyes. What
does their dreamy solemnity mean if not,
"the Lord hath smitten him by the hand
of a woman " ? One other delicate bit of
symbolising he has allowed himself, which
I may not omit. You are to see by whom
this deed was done : by a woman who has
unsexed herself. Judith is absorbed in her
awful service; her robe trails on the ground
and clings about her knees ; she is unconscious of the hindrance. The gates of
Bethulia are in sight, the Chaldean horsemen are abroad, but she has no anxiety to
escape. She is swift because her life just
now courses swiftly; but there is no haste.
The maid, you shall mark, picks up her
skirts with careful hand, and steps out the
more lustily for it.

So far Botticelli the poet, and so far also
Mr. Ruskin, reader of pictures. What says
Botticelli the painter ? Had he no instincts
to tell him that his art could have little to
say to a legend ? Or that a legend might

be the subject of an epic (here, indeed, was an epic ready made), might, under conditions, be the subject of a drama ; but could not, under any conditions, be alone the subject of a picture ? I don't for a moment suggest that he had, or that any artist ever goes to work in this double-entry, methodical way, but are we entitled to say that he was not influenced by his predilections, his determinations as a draughtsman, when he squared himself to illustrate the Bible ? We say that the subject of a picture is the spirit of natural fact. If Botticelli was a painter, *that* is what he must have looked for, and must have found, in every picture he painted. Where, then, was he to get his natural facts in the story of Judith ? What is, in that story, the natural, essential (as opposed to the historical, fleeting) fact ? It is murder. Judith's deed was what the old Scots law incisively calls *slauchter*. It may be glossed over as assassination or even execution—in fact, in Florence, where Giuliano was soon to be taken off, it did not fail to be so called : it remains, how-ever, just murder. Botticelli, not shirking the position at all, judged murder to be

a natural fact, and its spirit or essence
swiftness and stealth. Chaucer, let us
note, had been of the same mind :

" The smyler with the knyf under his cloke,"

and so on, in lines not to be matched for
hasty and dreadful suggestion. Swiftness
and stealth, the ambush, the averted face
and the sudden stab, are the standing elements of murder : pare off all the rest, you
come down to that. Your staring looks,
your blood, your "chirking," are accident-
als. They may be there (for each of us
carries a carcase), but the horror of sudden
death is above them : a man may strangle
with his thoughts clearer than with his
pair of hands. And as "matter" is but
the stuff wherewith Nature works, and
she is only insulted, not defied, when we
flout or mangle it, so it is against the high
dignity of Art to insist upon the carrion
she must use. She will press, here the
terror, there the radiance, of essential fact ;
she will leave to us, seeing it in her face,
to add mentally the poor stage properties
we have grown to trust. No blood, if you
please. Therefore, in Botticelli's *Judith,*
nothing but the essentials is insisted on ;

the rest we instantly imagine, but it is not
there to be sensed. The panel is in a
tremor. So swift and secret is Judith, so
furtive the maid, we need no hurrying
horsemen to remind us of her oath,—
"Hear me, and I will do a thing which
shall go throughout all generations to the
children of our nation." Sudden death is
in the air ; nature has been outraged. But
there is no drop of blood—the thin scarlet
line along the sword-edge is a symbol if
you will—the pale head in the cloth is a
mere "thing" : yet we all know what has
been done. Mr. Ruskin is wrong to dwell
here upon the heroism of the heroine, the
beneficence of the crime, the exhilaration
of the patriot ; he is traducing the painter
by so praising the poet. All those things
may be there ; and why should they not ?
But it is a pity to insist upon them until
you have no space for the pictorial something which is there too, and makes the
picture.

Other *Judiths* there are ; two here, one
next door in the Pitti, any number scattered
over the galleries of Europe. There are
Jacopo Palma of Venice and Allori of
Florence who used the old story, the one

to perpetuate a fat blonde, the other a handsome actress in a " strong " situation ; there
is Sodoma ; there are Horace Vernet and
the moderns, the Wests and Haydons of
our grandfathers. It is a pet subject of the
Salon. These men have vulgarised an epic,
and smirched poetry and painting alike
for the sake of a tawdry sensation. But
enough : let us look at one more. Mantegna's is worth looking at. It is a pen
drawing, often repeated, best known by
the fine engraving he finally made of it.
I think it is the best murder picture in the
world. To begin with, the literary interest
of the story is practically gone. This wild,
terrible, beautiful woman may be Judith if
you choose : she might be Medea or Agavè,
or Salome, or the Lucrezia Borgia of popular fancy and Donizetti. The fact is she
is part of a scheme whose object is the
æsthetic aspect of murder—murder considered as one of the fine arts. Andrea was
able, and I know not that anybody else
of his day could have been able, to con-
template murder purely objectively, with
no thought of its ethical relations. Botticelli had been fired by the heroism and the
moral grandeur of the special circumstances

of a given case : down they went into his picture with what rightly belonged to it. There is none of that here. And Mantegna makes other distinctions in the field common to both of them. Murder, for him, did not essentially subsist in its shocking suddenness ; it held something more specific, a witchery of its own, a *macabre* fascination, a mystery. Leonardo felt it when he drew his *Medusa ;* Shelley wrote it down "the tempestuous loveliness of terror." Thus it had, for Mantegna, an unique emotional habit which set it off from other vice and gave it a positive, appreciable, æsthetic value of its own. With even more unerrancy than Botticelli, he gripped the adjectival and qualifying function of his art. He saw that crime, too, had its pictorial side. When Keats, writing of the Lamia sloughing her snake-folds, tells us how—

" She writhed about, *convulsed with scarlet pain ;* "

or when, of organ music, he says—

" Up aloft
The silver, *snarling* trumpets 'gan to chide,"

he is simply, in his own art and with his proper methods, getting precisely the same kind of effect : he is incarnating the soul of a fact. ‵And so Mantegna, with his Roman kindness for whatever had breadth and vigour and boldness of design, carved his *Judith* on the lines of a Vestal Virgin, and gave her the rapt, dæmonic features of the Tragic Muse. And, with his full share of that unhealthy craving for the mere nastiness of crime, that Amina-trait which distinguished the later Empire and its correlate the Renaissance, he drew together the elements of his picture to express an eminently characteristic conception of curious murder. What amplitude of outline ; what severe grace of drapery ! And what mad affectation of attention to the ghastly baggage she is preparing for her flight ! ‵I can only instance for a parallel the pitiful case of the young Ophelia, decked with flowers and weeds, and faltering in her pretty treble songs about lechery and dead bodies. It needs strong men to do these things ; men who have lived out all that the world can offer them of heaven and hell, and, with the tolerance of maturity, are in the mind to see something worth a thought in either. There is in murder something more horrible than

blood,—the spirit that breeds blood and plays with it. M. Jan van Beers and his kindred of the dissecting-room and accidents'-ward are passed by Mantegna, who gives no vulgar illusion of gaping wounds and jetting blood ; but, instead, holds up to us a beautiful woman daintily fingering a corpse.

VII

I

UP at Fiesole, among the olives and chestnuts which cloud the steeps, the magnificent Lorenzo was entertaining his guests on a morning in April. The olives were just whitening to silver ; they stretched in a trembling sea down the slope. Beyond lay Florence, misty and golden; and round about were the mossy hills, cut sharp and definite against a grey-blue sky, printed with starry buildings and sober ranks of cypress. The sun, catching the mosaics of San Miniato and the brazen cross on the façade, made them shine like sword-blades in the quiver of the heat between. For the valley was just a lake of hot air, hot and murky—"fever weather," said the people in the streets—with a glaring summer sun let in between two long spells of fog. 'T was unnatural at that season, *via ;* but the blessed Saints sent the

114

weather, and one could only be careful what one was about at sun-down.

Up at the villa, with brisk morning airs rustling overhead, in the cool shades of trees and lawns, it was pleasant to lie still, watching these things, while a silky young exquisite sang to his lute a not too audacious ballad about Selvaggia, or Becchina and the saucy Prior of Sant' Onofrio. He sang well, too, that dark-eyed boy; the girl at whose feet he was crouched was laughing and blushing at once; and, being very fair, she blushed hotly. She dared not raise her eyes to look into his, and he knew it and was quietly measuring his strength—it was quite a comedy! At each wanton *refrain* he lowered his voice to a whisper and bent a little forward. And the girl's laughter became hysterical; she was shaking with the effort to control herself. At last she looked up with a sort of sob in her breath and saw his mocking smile and the gleam of the wild beast in his eyes. She grew white, rose hastily and turned away to join a group of ladies sitting apart. A man with a heavy, rather sullen face and a bush of yellow hair falling over his forehead in a wave was standing aside watching all this. He folded his arms and scowled under his big brows ; and when the girl moved away his eyes followed her.

The lad ended his song in a broad sarcasm amid bursts of laughter and applause. The Magnificent, sitting in his carved chair, nursed his sallow face and smiled approval. " My brother boasts his invulnerability," he said, turning to his neighbour ; "let him look to it, Messer Cupido will have him yet. Already, we can see, he has been let into some of the secrets of the bower." The man bowed and smiled deferentially. "Signor Giuliano has all the qualities to win the love of ladies, and to retain it. Doubtless he awaits his destiny. The Wise Man has said that ' Beauty . . .'" The young poet enlarged on his text with some fire in his thin cheeks, while the company kept very silent. It was much to their liking ; even Giuliano was absorbed; he sat on the ground clasping one knee between his hands, smiling upwards into vacancy, as a man does whose imagination is touched. Lorenzo nursed his sallow face and beat time to the orator's cadences with his foot ; he, too, was abstracted and smiling. At the end he spoke: "Our

Marsilio himself has never said nobler words, my Agnolo. The mantle of the Attic prophet has descended indeed upon this Florence. And Beauty, as thou sayest, is from heaven. But where shall it be found here below, and how discerned?" The man of the heavy jowl was standing with folded arms, looking from under his brows at the group of girls. Lorenzo saw everything; he noticed him. "Our Sandro will tell us it is yonder. The Star of Genoa shines over Florence and our poor little constellations are gone out. *Ecco*, my Sandro, gravest and hardiest of painters, go summon Madonna Simonetta and her handmaidens to our Symposium. Agnolo will speak further to us of this sovereignty of Beauty."

The painter bowed his head and moved away.

A green alley vaulted with thick ilex and myrtle formed a tapering vista where the shadows lay misty blue and pale shafts of light pierced through fitfully. At the far end it ran out into an open space and a splash of sunshine. A marble Ganymede with lifted arms rose in the middle like a white flame. The girls were there, intent upon some commerce of their own, flashing hither and thither over the grass in a flutter of saffron and green and crimson. Simonetta—Sandro could see—was a little apart, a very tall, isolated figure, clear and cold in a recess of shade, standing easily, resting on one hip with her hands behind her. A soft, straight robe of white clipped her close from shoulder to heel; the lines of her figure were thrust forward by her poise. His eye followed the swell of her bosom, very gentle and girlish, and the long folds of her dress falling thence to her knee. While she stood there, proud and remote, a chance beam of the sun shone on her head so that it seemed to burn. "Heaven salutes the Queen of Heaven,—Venus Urania!" With an odd impulse he stopped, crossed himself, and then hurried on.

He told his errand to her, having no eyes for the others.

"Signorina—I am to acquaint her Serenity that the divine poet Messer Agnolo is to speak of the sovereign power of beauty; of the Heavenly Beauty whereof Plato taught, as it is believed."

Simonetta arched a slim neck and looked down at the obsequious speaker, or at least he thought so. And he saw how fair she was, a creature how delicate and gracious, with grey eyes frank and wide, and full red lips where a smile (nervous and a little wistful, he judged, rather than defiant) seemed always to hover. Such clear-cut, high beauty made him ashamed; but her colouring (for he was a painter) made his heart beat. She was no ice-bound shadow of deity then ! but flesh and blood ; a girl —a child, of timid, soft contours, of warm roses and blue veins laced in a pearly skin. And she was crowned with a heavy wealth of red-gold hair, twisted in great coils, bound about with pearls, and smouldering like molten metal where it fell rippling along her neck. She dazzled him, so that he could not face her or look further. His eyes dropped. He stood before her moody, disconcerted.

The girls, who had dissolved their company at his approach, listened to what he had to say linked in knots of twos and threes. They needed no excuses to return; some were philosophers in their way, philosophers and poetesses ; some had left their lovers in the ring round Lorenzo. So they went down the green alley still locked by the arms, by the waist or shoulders. They did not wait for Simonetta. She was a Genoese, and proud as the snow. Why did Giuliano love her? *Did* he love her, indeed? He was bewitched then, for she was cold, and a brazen creature in spite of it. How dare she bare her neck so! Oh! 't was Genoese. "Uomini senza fede e donne senza vergogna," they quoted as they ran.

And Simonetta walked alone down the way with her head high; but Sandro stepped behind, at the edge of her trailing white robe. . . .

. . . The poet was leaning against an ancient alabaster vase, soil-stained, yellow with age and its long sojourn in the loam, but with traces of its carved garlands clinging to it still. He fingered it lovingly as he talked. His oration was concluding, and his voice rose high and tremulous; there were sparks in his hollow eyes. . . . "And as this sovereign Beauty is queen of herself, so she is subject to none other, owns to no constraining custom, fears no reproach of man. What she wills, that has the force of a law. Being Beauty, her deeds are lovely and worshipful. Therefore

Phrynè, whom men, groping in darkness and the dull ways of earth, dubbed
courtesan, shone in a Court of Law before
the assembled nobles of Athens, naked and
undismayed in the blaze of her fairness.
And Athens discerned the goddess and
trembled. Yes, and more; even as Aph-
rodite, whose darling she was, arose pure
from the foam, so she too came up out of
the sea in the presence of a host, and the
Athenians, seeing no shame, thought
none, but, rather, reverenced her the more.
For what shame is it that the body of one
so radiant in clear perfections should be
revealed ? Is then the garment of the soul,
her very mould and image, so shameful ?
Shall we seek to know her essence by the
garment of a garment, or hope to behold
that which really is in the shadows we cast
upon shadows ? Shame is of the brute
dullard who thinks shame. The evil ever
sees Evil glaring at him. Plato, the golden-
mouthed, with the soul of pure fire, has
said the truth of this matter in his *De Re-
publicâ*, the fifth book, where he speaks of
young maids sharing the exercise of the
Palæstra, yea, and the Olympic contests
even! For he says, ' Let the wives of our

wardens bare themselves, for their virtue will be a robe ; and let them share the toils of war and defend their country. And for the man who laughs at naked women exercising their bodies for high reasons, his laughter is a fruit of unripe wisdom, and he himself knows not what he is about; for that is ever the best of sayings that ' the useful is the noble and the hurtful the base.' . . ."

There was a pause. The name of Plato had had a strange effect upon the company. You would have said they had suddenly entered a church and had felt all lighter interests sink under the weight of the dim, echoing nave. After a few moments the poet spoke again in a quieter tone, but his voice had lost none of the unction which had enriched it. . . . " Beauty is queen: by the virtue of Deity, whose image she is, she reigns, lifts up, fires. Let us beware how we tempt Deity lest we perish ourselves. Actæon died when he gazed unbidden upon the pure body of Artemis ; but Artemis herself rayed her splendour upon Endymion, and Endymion is among the immortals. We fall when we rashly confront Beauty, but that Beauty who comes unawares may nerve our souls to wing to heaven." He ended on a resonant note, and then, still looking out over the valley, sank into his seat. Lorenzo, with a fine humility, got up and kissed his thin hand. Giuliano looked at Simonetta, trying to recall her gaze, but she remained standing in her place, seeing nothing of her companions. She was thinking of something, frowning a little and biting her lip ; her hands were before her; her slim fingers twisted and locked themselves nervously, like a tangle of snakes. Then she tossed her head, as a young horse might, and looked at Giuliano suddenly, full in the eyes. He rose to meet her with a deprecating smile, cap in hand—but she walked past him, almost brushing him with her gown, but never flinching her full gaze, threaded her way through the group to the back, behind the poet, where Sandro was. He had seen her coming, indeed he had watched her furtively throughout the oration, but her near presence disconcerted him again—and he looked down. She was strongly excited with her quick resolution ; her colour had risen and her voice faltered when she began to speak.

She spoke eagerly, running her words together.

" *Ecco*, Messer Sandro," she whispered, blushing. " You have heard these sayings. . . . Who is there in Florence like me ? "

"There is no one," said Sandro, simply.

"I will be your Lady Venus," she went on, breathlessly. "You shall paint me, rising from the sea-foam. . . . The Genoese love the sea." She was still eager and defiant ; her bosom rose and fell unchecked.

"The Signorina is mocking me; it is impossible; the Signorina knows it."

" Eh, *Madonna !* is it so shameful to be fair—Star of the Sea, as your poets sing at evening ? Do you mean that I dare not do it ? Listen then, Signor Pittore; to-morrow morning at mass-time you will come to the Villa Vespucci with your brushes and pans and you will ask for Monna Simonetta. Then you will see. Leave it now ; it is settled." And she walked away with her head high and the same superb smile on her red lips. Mockery ! She was in dead earnest; all her child's feelings were in hot revolt. These women who had whispered to each other, sniggered at her dress, her white neck and her free carriage ; Giuliano, who had presumed so upon her candour—these prying, censorious Florentines—she would strike them dumb with her amazing loveliness. They sang her a goddess that she might be flattered and suffer their company: she would show herself a goddess indeed—the star of her shining Genoa, where men were brave and silent and maidens frank like the sea. Yes, and then she would withdraw herself suddenly and leave them forlorn and dismayed.

As for Sandro, he stood where she had left him, peering after her with a mist in his eyes. He seemed to be looking over the hill-side, over the city glowing afar off gold and purple in the hot air, to Mont' Oliveto and the heights, where a line of black cypresses stood about a low white building. At one angle of the building was a little turret with a belvedere of round arches. The tallest cypresses just topped the windows. There his eyes seemed to rest.

II

At mass-time Sandro, folded in his shabby

green cloak, stepped into the sun on the Ponte Vecchio. The morning mists were rolling back under the heat; you began to see the yellow line of houses stretching along the turbid river on the far side, and frowning down upon it with blank, mud-stained faces. Above, through streaming air, the sky showed faintly blue, and a *campanile* to the right loomed pale and uncertain like a ghost. The sound of innumerable bells floated over the still city. Hardly a soul was abroad; here and there a couple of dusty peasants were trudging in with baskets of eggs and jars of milk and oil; a boat passed down to the fishing, and the oar knocked sleepily in the rowlock as she cleared the bridge. And above, on the heights of Mont' Oliveto, the tapering forms of cypresses were faintly outlined—straight bars of shadow—and the level ridge of a roof ran lightly back into the soft shroud.

Sandro could mark these things as he stepped resolutely on to the bridge, crossed it, and went up a narrow street among the sleeping houses. The day held golden promise; it was the day of his life! Meanwhile the mist clung to him and nipped him; what had fate in store? What was to be the issue? In the Piazza Santo Spirito, grey and hollow-sounding in the chilly silences, his own footsteps echoed solemnly as he passed by the door of the great ragged church. Through the heavy darkness within lights flickered faintly and went; service was not begun. A drab crew of cripples lounged on the steps yawning and shivering, and two country girls were strolling to mass with brown arms round each other's waists. When Sandro's footfall clattered on the stones they stopped by the door, looking after him, and laughed to see his dull face and muffled figure. In the street beyond he heard a bell jingling, hasty, incessant; soon a white-robed procession swept by him, fluttering vestments, tapers, and the Host under a canopy, silk and gold. Sandro snatched at his cap and dropped on his knees in the road, crouching low and muttering under his breath as the vision went past. He remained kneeling for a moment after it had gone, then crossed himself— forehead, breast, lip—and hurried forward. . . . He stepped under the archway into the court. There was a youth with a cropped head and swarthy neck lounging there teazing a spaniel. As the steps sounded on the flags he looked up; the old green cloak and clumsy shoes of the visitor did not interest him; he turned his back and went on with his game. Sandro accosted him—Was the Signorina at the house? The boy went on with his game. "Eh, Diavolo! I know nothing at all," he said.

Sandro raised his voice till it rang round the courtyard. "You will go at once and inquire. You will say to the Signorina that Sandro di Mariano Filipepi the Florentine painter is here by her orders ; that he waits her pleasure below."

The boy had got up ; he and Sandro eyed each other for a little space. Sandro was the taller and had the glance of a hawk. So the porter went. . . . Presently, with throbbing brows, he stood on the threshold of Simonetta's chamber. It was the turret room of the villa and its four arched windows looked through a leafy tracery over towards Florence. Sandro could see down below him in the haze the glitter of the Arno and the dusky dome of Brunelleschi cleave the sward of the hills like a great burnished

128

bowl. In the room itself there was tapestry, the Clemency of Scipio, with courtiers in golden cuirasses and tall plumes, and peacocks and huge Flemish horses—a rich profusion of crimson and blue drapery and stout-limbed soldiery. On a bracket, above a green silk curtain, was a silver statuette of Madonna and the Bambino Gesù, with a red lamp flickering feebly before ; by the windows a low divan heaped with velvet cushions and skins. But for a coffer and a prayer desk and a curtained recess which enshrined Simonetta's bed, the room looked wind-swept and bare.

When he entered Simonetta was standing by the window leaning her hand against the ledge for support. She was draped from top to toe in a rose-coloured mantle which shrouded her head like a nun's wimple and then fell in heavy folds to the ground. She flushed as he came in, but saluted him with a grave inclination. Neither spoke. The silent greeting, the full consciousness in each of their parts, gave a curious religious solemnity to the scene —like some familiar but stately Church mystery. Sandro busied himself mechanically with his preparations — he was a lover and his pulse chaotic, but he had come to paint—and when these were done, on tip-toe, as it were, he looked timidly about him round the room, seeking where to pose her. Then he motioned her with the same reverential, preoccupied air, silent still, to a place under the silver Madonna. . . .

. . . There was a momentary quiver of withdrawal. Simonetta blushed vividly and drooped her eyes down to her little bare feet peeping out below the lines of the rosy cloak. The cloak's warmth shone on her smooth skin and rayed over her cheeks. In her flowery loveliness she looked diaphanous, ethereal ; and yet you could see what a child she was, with her bright audacity, her ardour and her wilful-ness flushing and paling about her like the dawn. There she stood trembling on the brink. . . .

Suddenly all her waywardness shot into her eyes ; she lifted her arms and the cloak fell back like the shard of a young flower ; then, delicate and palpitating as a silver reed, she stood up in the soft light of the morn-ing, and the sun, slanting in between the golden leaves and tendrils, kissed her neck and shrinking shoulder.

Sandro stood facing her, moody and troubled, fingering his brushes and bits of charcoal; his shaggy brows were knit, he seemed to be breathing hard. He collected himself with an effort and looked up at her as she stood before him shrinking, awe-struck, panting at the thing she had done. Their eyes met, and the girl's distress in-creased; she raised her hand to cover her bosom; her breath came in short gasps from parted lips, but her wide eyes still looked fixedly into his, with such blank panic that a sudden movement might really have killed her. He saw it all; she, there at his mercy! Tears swam and he trem-bled. Ah! the gracious lady! what divine condescension! what ineffable cour-tesy! But the artist in him was awak-ened almost at the same moment; his looks wandered in spite of her piteous candour and his own nothingness. Sandro the poet would have fallen on his face with an "Exi a me, nam peccator sum." San-dro the painter was different—no mercy there. He made a snatch at a carbon and raised his other hand with a kind of com-mand—"Holy Virgin! what a line! Stay as you are, I implore you: swerve not one

hair's breadth and I have you for ever!"
There was conquest in his voice.

So Simonetta stood very still, hiding her
bosom with her hand, but never took her
watch off the enemy. As he ran blindly
about doing a hundred urgent indispensa-
ble things,—noting the lights, the line she
made, how her arm cut across the folds of
the curtain—she dogged him with staring,
fascinated eyes, just as a hare, crouching in
her form, watches a terrier hunting round
her and waits for the end.

But the enemy was disarmed. Sandro
the passionate, the lover, the brooding de-
votee, was gone; so was *la bella Simonetta*
the beloved, the be-hymned. Instead,
here was a fretful painter, dashing lines
and broad smudges of shade on his paper,
while before him rose an exquisite, slender,
swaying form, glistening carnation and silver, and, over all, the maddening glow of
red-gold hair. Could he but catch those
velvet shadows, those delicate, glossy, re-
flected lights! Body of Bacchus! How
could he put them in! What a picture
she was! Look at the sun on her shoulder!
and her hair—Christ! how it burned! It
was a curious moment. The girl, who had

never understood or cared to understand this humble lover, guessed now that he was lost in the artist. She felt that she was simply an effect, and she resented it as a crowning insult. Her colour rose again, her red lips gathered into a pout. If Sandro had but known, she was his at that instant. He had but to drop the painter, throw down his brushes, set his heart and hot eyes bare—to open his arms and she would have fled into them and nestled there; so fierce was her instinct just then to be loved, she, who had always been loved! But Sandro knew nothing and cared nothing. He was absorbed in the gracious lines of her body, the lithe long neck, the drooping shoulder, the tenderness of her youth; and then the grand open curve of the hip and thigh on which she was poised. He drew them in with a free hand in great sweeping lines, eagerly, almost angrily; once or twice he broke his carbon and— body of a dog !—he snatched at another.

This lasted a few minutes only : even Simonetta, with all her maiden tremors still feverishly acute, hardly noticed the flight of time ; she was so hot with the feeling of her wrongs, the slight upon her victorious

fairness. Did she not *know* how fair
she was? She was getting very angry ;
she had been made a fool of. All Florence
would come and gape at the picture and
mock her in the streets with bad names
and coarse gestures as she rode by. She
looked at Sandro. Santa Maria ! how hot
he was ! His hair was drooping over his
eyes ! He tossed it back every second !
And his mouth was open, one could see
his tongue working ! Why had she not
noticed that great mouth before ? 'T was
the biggest in all Florence. Oh ! why had
he come ? She was frightened, remorseful,
a child again, with a trembling, pathetic
mouth and shrinking limbs. And then her
heart began to beat under her slim fingers.
She pressed them down into her flesh to
stay those great, masterful throbs. A tear
gathered in her eye ; larger and larger it
grew, and then fell. A shining drop rested
on the round of her cheek and rolled slowly
down her chin to her protecting hand, and
lay there half-hidden, shining like a rain-
drop between two curving petals of a rose.

It was just at that moment the painter
looked up from his work and shook his
bush of hair back. Something in his sketch

had displeased him ; he looked up frowning, with a brush between his teeth. When he saw the tear-stained, distressful, beautiful face it had a strange effect upon him. He dropped nerveless, like a wounded man, to his knees, and covered his eyes with his hands. "Ah Madonna ! for the pity of heaven forgive me ! forgive me ! I have sinned, I have done thee fearful wrong ; I, who still dare to love thee." He uncovered his face and looked up radiant ; his own words had inspired him. "Yes," he went on, with a steadfast smile, "I, Sandro, the painter, the poor devil of a painter, have seen thee and I dare to love !" His triumph was short-lived. Simonetta had grown deadly white, her eyes burned, she had forgotten herself. She was tall and slender as a lily, and she rose, shaking, to her height.

"Thou presumest strangely," she said, in a slow, still voice, "Go ! Go in peace !"

She was conqueror. In her calm scorn, she was like a young immortal, some cold, victorious Cynthia whose chastity had been flouted. Sandro was pale too ; he said nothing and did not look at her again. She stood quivering with excitement, watching

him with the same intent alertness as he
rolled up his paper and crammed his
brushes and pencils into the breast of his
jacket. She watched him still as he backed
out of the room and disappeared through
the curtains of the archway. She listened
to his footsteps along the corridor, down
the stair. She was alone in the silence of
the sunny room. Her first thought was for
her cloak ; she snatched it up and veiled
herself, shivering as she looked fearfully
round the walls. And then she flung herself on the piled cushions before the window
and sobbed piteously, like an abandoned
child.

The sun slanted in between the golden
leaves and tendrils and played in the tangle
of her hair. . . .

III

At ten o'clock on the morning of April
the twenty-sixth, a great bell began to toll :
two beats heavy and slow, and then silence,
while the air echoed the reverberation,
moaning. Sandro, in shirt and breeches,
with bare feet spread broad, was at work
in his garret on the old bridge. He stayed
his hand as the strong tone struck, bent his

head and said a prayer : "Miserere ei, Domine ; requiem eternam dona, Domine " ;
the words came out of due order, as if he
was very conscious of their import. Then
he went on. And the great bell went on ;
two beats together, and then silence. It
seemed to gather solemnity and a heavier
message as he painted. Through the open
window a keen draught of air blew in with
dust and a scrap of shaving from the Lung'
Arno down below ; it circled round his
workshop, fluttering the sketches and rags
pinned to the walls. He looked out on a
bleak landscape — San Miniato in heavy
shade, and the white houses by the river
staring like dead faces. A strong breeze
was abroad ; it whipped the brown water
and raised little curling billows, ragged and
white at the edges, and tossed about snaps
of surf. It was cold. Sandro shivered as
he shut to his casement ; and the stiffening
gale rattled at it fitfully. Once again it
thrust it open, bringing wild work among
the litter in the room. He made it fast with
the rain driving in his face. And above
the howling of the squall he heard the
sound of the great bell, steady and un-
moved, as if too full of its message to be

put aside. Yet it was coming to him athwart the wind.

Sandro stood at his casement and looked at the weather—beating rain and yeasty water. He counted, rather nervously, the pulses between each pair of the bell's deep tones. He was impressionable to circumstances, and the coincidence of storm and passing-bell awed him. . . . " Either the God of Nature suffers or the fabric of the world is breaking " ;—he remembered a scrap of talk wafted towards him (as he stood in attendance) from some humanist at Lorenzo's table only yesterday, above the light laughter and snatches of song. That breakfast party at the Camaldoli yesterday ! What a contrast—the even spring weather with the sun in a cloudless sky, and now this icy dead morning with its battle of wind and bell, fighting, he thought,—over the failing breath of some strong man. Man ! God, more like. "The God of Nature suffers," he murmured, as he turned to his work. . . .

Simonetta had not been there yesterday. He had not seen her, indeed, since that nameless day when she had first transported him with the radiance of her bare beauty and then struck him down with a level gaze from steel-cold eyes. And he had deserved it, he had—she had said—"presumed strangely." Three more words only had she uttered and he had slunk out from her presence like a dog. What a Goddess! Venus Urania! So she, too, might have ravished a worshipper as he prayed, and, after, slain him for a careless word. Cruel? No, but a Goddess. Beauty had no laws ; she was above them. Agnolo himself had said it, from Plato. . . . Holy Michael ! What a blast ! Black and desperate weather. . . . "Either the God of Nature suffers." . . . God shield all Christian souls on such a day ! . . .

One came and told him Simonetta Vespucci was dead. Some fever had torn at her and raced through all her limbs, licking up her life as it passed. No one had known of it—it was so swift ! But there had just been time to fetch a priest ; Fra Matteo, they said, from the Carmine, had shrived her (it was a bootless task, God knew, for the child had babbled so, her wits wandered, look you), and then he had performed the last office. One had fled to

tell the Medici. Giuliano was wild with
grief ; 't was as if *he* had killed her instead
of the Spring-ague—but then, people said
he loved her well ! And our Lorenzo had
bid them swing the great bell of the Duomo
—Sandro had heard it perhaps ?—and there
was to be a public procession, and a Requiem sung at Santa Croce before they took
her back to Genoa to lie with her fathers.
Eh ! Bacchus ! She was fair and Giuliano
had loved her well. It was natural enough
then. So the gossip ran out to tell his
news to more attentive ears, and Sandro
stood in his place intoning softly "Te
Deum Laudamus."

He understood it all. There had been a
dark and awful strife—earth shuddering as
the black shadow of death swept by.
Through tears now the sun beamed broad
over the gentle city where she lay lapped in
her mossy hills. "Lux eterna lucet ei," he
said, with a steady smile; "atque lucebit,"
he added after a pause. He had been painting that day an agonizing Christ, red and
languid, crowned with thorns. Some of his
own torment seems to have entered it, for,
looking at it now, we see, first of all, wild
eyeballs staring with the mad earnestness,

the purposeless intensity of one seized or "possessed." He put the panel away and looked about for something else, the sketch he had made of Simonetta on that last day. When he had found it, he rolled it straight and set it on his easel. It was not the first charcoal study he had made from life, but a brush drawing on dark paper, done in sepia-wash and the lights in white lead. He stood looking into it with his hands clasped. About half a braccia high, faint and shadowy in the pale tint he had used, he saw her there victim rather than Goddess. Standing timidly and wistfully, shrinking rather, veiling herself, maiden-like, with her hands and hair, with lips trembling and dewy eyes, she seemed to him now an immortal who must needs suffer for some great end; live and suffer and die; live again, and suffer and die. It was a doom perpetual like Demeter's, to bear, to nurture, to lose and to find her Persephone. She had stood there immaculate and apprehensive, a wistful victim. Three days before he had seen her thus ; and now she was dead. He would see her no more.

Ah, yes! Once more he would see
her. . . .

. . . . . .

They carried dead Simonetta through the
streets of Florence with her pale face uncovered and a crown of myrtle in her hair.
People thronging there held their breath
or wept to see such still loveliness; and
her poor parted lips wore a patient little
smile, and her eyelids were pale violet and
lay heavy to her cheek. White, like a
bride, with a nosegay of orange-blossom
and syringa at her throat, she lay there on
her bed with lightly folded hands and the
strange aloofness and preoccupation all
the dead have. Only her hair burned about
her like a molten copper; and the wreath
of myrtle leaves ran forward to her brows
and leapt beyond them into a tongue.

The great procession swept forward;
black brothers of Misericordia, shrouded
and awful, bore the bed or stalked before it
with torches that guttered and flared sootily
in the dancing light of day. They held
the pick of Florence, those scowling shrouds
—Giuliano and Lorenzo, Pazzi, Tornabuoni,
Soderini or Pulci; and behind, old Cat-
taneo, battered with storms, walked

heavily, swinging his long arms and looking into the day's face as if he would try
another fall with Death yet. Priests and
acolytes, tapers, banners, vestments and a
great silver Crucifix, they drifted by,
chanting the dirge for Simonetta; and she,
as if for a sacrifice, lifted up on her silken
bed, lay couched like a white flower edged
colour of flame. . . .

. . . Santa Croce, the great church,
stretched forward beyond her into the dis-
tances of grey mist and cold spaces of light.
Its bare vastness was damp like a vault.
And she lay in the midst listless, heavy-lidded, apart, with the half-smile, as it
seemed, of some secret mirth. Round her
the great candles smoked and flickered,
and mass was sung at the High Altar for
her soul's repose. Sandro stood alone
facing the shining altar, but looking fixedly
at Simonetta on her couch. He was white
and dry—parched lips and eyes that ached
and smarted. Was this the end ? Was it
possible, my God ! that the transparent,
unearthly thing lying there so prone and
pale was dead ? Had such loveliness aught
to do with life or death ? Ah! sweet lady,
dear heart, how tired she was, how deadly

tired! From where he stood he could see with intolerable anguish the sombre rings round her eyes and the violet shadows on the lids, her folded hands and the straight, meek line to her feet. And her poor wan face with its wistful, pitiful little smile was turned half aside on the delicate throat, as if in a last appeal:—"Leave me now, O Florentines, to my rest. I have given you all I had: ask no more. I was a young girl, a child; too young for your eager strivings. You have killed me with your play; let me be now, let me sleep!" Poor child! Poor child! Sandro was on his knees, with his face pressed against the pulpit and tears running through his fingers as he prayed. . . .

As he had seen her, so he painted. As at the beginning of life in a cold world, passively meeting the long trouble of it, he painted her a rapt Presence floating evenly to our earth. A grey, translucent sea laps silently upon a little creek, and in the hush of a still dawn the myrtles and sedges on the water's brim are quiet. It is a dream in half tones that he gives us, grey and green and steely blue ; and just that, and some homely magic of his own, hint the

ANADYOMENÊ

commerce of another world with man's discarded domain. Men and women are asleep, and as in an early walk you may startle the hares at their play, or see the creatures of the darkness—owls and night hawks and heavy moths—flit with fantastic purpose over the familiar scene, so here it comes upon you suddenly that you have surprised Nature's self at her mysteries ; you are let into the secret; you have caught the spirit of the April woodland as she glides over the pasture to the copse. And that, indeed, was Sandro's fortune. He caught her in just such a propitious hour. He saw the sweet wild thing, pure and undefiled by touch of earth; caught her in that pregnant pause of time ere she had lighted. Another moment and a buxom nymph of the grove would fold her in a rosy mantle, coloured as the earliest wood-anemones are. She would vanish, we know, into the daffodils or a bank of violets. And you might tell her presence there, or in the rustle of the myrtles, or coo of doves mating in the pines; you might feel her genius in the scent of the earth or the kiss of the West wind; but you could only see her in mid-April, and you should look for her over the sea. She always comes with the first warmth of the year.

But daily, before he painted, Sandro knelt in a dark chapel in Santa Croce, while a blue-chinned priest said mass for the repose of Simonetta's soul.

VIII

THE BURDEN OF NEW TYRE

FOR a short time in her motley history,
an old-clothesman, one Domenico—
he and his "Compagnia del Bruco," his
Company of the Worm *—reigned over
Siena and gave to her people a taste for
blood. It was a bloodshed on easy terms
they had ; for surely no small nation (except that tiger-cat Perugia) has achieved
so much massacre with so little fighting.
Massacre considered as one of the Fine
Arts ? No indeed ; but massacre as a *via-
ticum*, as "title clear to mansions in the
skies" ; for, with more complacency than
discrimination, these sated citizens chose
to dedicate their most fantastic blood-orgies
by a *Missa de Spiritu Sancto* in the Cathe-
dral Church. The old-clothesman, who by
some strange oversight died in his bed,
was floated up on the incense of this devout service to show his hands, and—

* This was one of the *Contrade* into which the City
was divided, and of which each had its totem-sign.

147

marvel!—Saint Catherine, the "amorosa sposa" of Heaven, reigned in his stead. Certainly, for unction spiced with ferocity, for a madness which alternately kissed the Crucifix and trampled on it, for mandragora and *fleurs de lys*, saints and succubi, churches and lupanars—commend me to Siena the red.

You are not to suppose that she has not paid for all this, the red Siena. None of it is absolved ; it is there floating vaguely in the atmosphere. It chokes the gully-trap streets in August when the air is like a hot bath ; it wails round the corners on stormy nights and you hear it battling among the towers overhead, buffeting the stained walls of criminal old palaces and churches grown hoary in iniquity—so many half-embodied centuries of deadly sin gnawing their spleens or shrieking their infamous carouse over again. So, at least, I found it. Without baring myself to the charge of any sneaking kindness for blood-shedding, I may own to the fascination of the precipitous fortress-town huddled red and grey on its three red crags, and of its suggestion of all the old crimes of Italy from Ezzelino's to Borgia's, of all unhappy

deaths from Pia de' Tolomei's to Vittoria's,
the White Devil of Italy. Its air seemed
"blood-boltered" (like the shade of the
hunted Banquo), its stones, curiously
slippery for such dry weather, cried
" Haro ! " or " Out ! Havoc ! " And above
it all shone a marble church, white as a
bride ; while now and again on a favour-
able waft of wind came the fragrant memory of Saint Catherine. It is the peak of
earth most charged with wayward emotions—pity and terror blent together into a
poignant beauty, a sorcery. Imagine yourself one of those old Popes—Linus or
Anaclete or Damasius—whose heads spike
the clerestory of the Duomo, you would
look down upon a sea of pictures (by the
best pavement-artists in the world)—the
Massacre of the Innocents like a patch of dry
blood by the altar-steps, a winking Madonna in the Capella del Voto thronged
with worshippers, Hermes Trismegistus,
a freaksome wizard, by the West door,
and a gilded array of the great world smiling and debonnair in the sacristy. Not far
off is Sodoma's lovely Catherine fainting
under the sweet dolour of her spousals.
Are you for the White or the Black Mass ?

Cybelè or the Holy Ghost ? Catherine or Hermes Trismegistus ? Siena will give you any and yet more cunning confections. It is very strange.

The approach to her three hills, if you are not flattened by the intolerable pilgrimage from Florence, is fine. Hints of what is to come greet you in the frittered shale of the grey country-side broken abruptly by little threatening hill-towns. The scar juts out of the earth's crust, rising sheer, and there on a fretted peak hovers a fortress-village, steep red roofs, an ancient bell-tower or two with a lean barrel of a church beyond ; all the lines cut sharp to the clean sky ; a bullock cart creaking up homewards ; the shiver and dust of olives round the walls. You could swear you caught the glint of a long gun over the machicolations ; but it is only a casement fired by the westering sun. Such are San Miniato, Castel Fiorentino, Poggibonsi (where stayed Lorenzo's Nencia—his Nancy, we should call her), San Gimignano and its Fina, a little girl-saint of fifteen springs ; such, too, is Siena when you get there, but redder, her grey stones blushing for her sins. And the country blushes for her as you draw near, for all the vineyards are dotted with burning willows in the autumn—osier-bushes flaming at the heart. Let it be night when you arrive—the dead vast and middle of a still night. Then suffer yourself to be whirled through the inky streets, over the flags, from one hill to another. It is deathly quiet ; no soul stirs. The palaces rise on either hand like the ghosts of old reproaches ; a flickering lamp reveals a gully as black as a grave, and shines on the edge of a lane which falls you know not whither. You turn corners which should complicate a maze, you scrape and clatter down steeps, you groan up mountainsides. All in the dark, mind. And the great white houses slide down upon you to the very flags you are beating ; you could nearly touch either wall with a hand. So you swerve round a column, under a votive lamp, and have left the stars and their violet bed. You are in a *cortile :* men say there is an inn here with reasonable entertainment. If it is the *Aquila Nera* it will serve. There is no sound beyond the labouring of our horses' wind and of some outland dog in the far distance baying for a moon. This is Siena at her black magic.

I maintain that the impression you thus receive holds you. Next morning there is a blare of sun. It will blind you at first, blister you. Rayed out from plaster-walls which have been soaking in it for five centuries, driven up in palpable waves of heat from the flags, lying like a lake of white metal in the Piazza, however recklessly this truly royal sun may beam, in Siena you will feel furtive and astare for sudden death.

There is nothing frank and open about Siena ; none of your robust, red-lunged, open-air Paganism. Théophile Gautier, Baudelaire, Poe — such super-sensitive plants should have known it, instead of the ingenuous M. Bourget and the deliberate Mr. Henry James. M. Bourget looked at the Sodomas and Mr. James admired the view: what a romance we should have had from Gautier of illicit joys and their requital by a knife, what a strophe from Baudelaire half-obscene, half-mournful, wholly melodious. But Théophile Gautier tarried in Venice, and as for M. Charles, the man of pronounced tastes and keen nose stuck in the main to Paris. Failing them as guides, go you first to the

Piazza del Campo where horses race in August—all roads lead thither.   Contraries again !   A square ?   It is a cup.   A field ? It is a Gabbatha: a place of burning pavements.   Were red brick and Gothic ever so superbly compounded before, to be so strong and yet so lithe ?   That is the Palazzo Publico, the shrine of Aristotle's *Politics* and the *Miracles of the Virgin*.   What is that long spear which seems to shake as it glances skywards ?   It isn't a spear; it's the Torre del Mangia —the loveliest tower in Tuscany, the *filia pulchrior* of a beautiful mother, the Torre della Vacca of Florence.   That tower rises from the bottom of the cup and shoots straight upwards, nor stays till it has out-topped the proudest belfry on the hills about it.   But what a square this is !   The backs of the houses (whose front doors are high above on

153

the hill-top) stand like bald cliffs on every side. You cannot see any outlets: most of them are winding stairways cut between the houses. The lounging, shabby men and girls seem handsomer and lazier than you found them in Florence. They seem to have room to stretch their fine limbs against these naked walls. Their maturity is almost tropical. The girls wear flopping straw hats : wide, sorrowful eyes stare at you from the shady recesses, and the rounding of their chins and beautiful proud necks are marked by glossy lights. "Morbida e bianca," sang Lorenzo. I suppose they think of little more than the market price of spring onions : but then, why do their eyes speak like that? And what do they speak of ? *Dio mio,* I am an honest man ! So was not Lorenzo ; listen to him :

> " Two eyes hath she, so roguish and demure
> That, lit they on a rock, they 'd make it feel ;
> How shall poor melting men meet such a lure ? "

How indeed ? Ah, Nenciozza mia !

> " My little Nancy shows nor fleck nor pimple ;
> Pliant and firm is she, a reed for grace :
> In her smooth chin there 's just one pretty dimple
> That rounds the perfect measure of her face. "

That dimple has been the destruction of many a heart:—

" So wise, withal, above us other simple
Plain folk—sure, Nature set her in this place
To bloom her tender whiteness all about us,
And break our hearts—and then bloom on without
us."

Yes indeed, my Lorenzo. But enough ! Let us take shelter in the Duomo.

Barred like a tiger, glistening snow and rose and gold, topped by a flaunting angel, her door flanked by the lean Roman wolf ; paved with pictures, hemmed with the Popes from Peter to Pius, encrusted with marbles and gemmy frescoes, it is a casket of delights, this church, and the quintessence of Siena—*molles Senæ* as Beccadelli, himself of this Tyre, dubbed his native town. Voluptuous as she was, tigerish Siena was more consistent than you would think. True, Saints Catherine and Bernardine consort oddly with the old-clothesman saying mass with wet hands, and Beccadelli the soft singer of abominations, just as the " Madones aux longs regards " of the Primitives—pious creatures of slim idle fingers and desirous eyes, pining in brocade and jewels—seem in a different sphere (as indeed they are) from Pinturricchio's well-found Popes and Princesses, and Sodoma's languishing boys or half-ripe Catherines dying of love. Have I not said this was once a city of pleasure? And whether the pleasure was a blood-feast or an *Agapè*, or a Platonic banquet where the flute-players and wine-cups and crowns crushed out the high disquisition and philosophic undercurrent —it was all one to soft Siena drowsing the days out on her hills. Her pleasures were fierce, and beautiful as fierce. But the burden of Tyre is always the same. And so the memories of a thousand ancient wrongs unpurged howl over the red city, as once howled the ships of Tarshish.

IX

GREATEST of great ladies is Ilaria,
potens Luccæ, sleeping easily, with
chin firmly rounded to the vault, where
she has slept for five hundred years, and
still a power in Lucca of the silver planes.
It was a white-hot September day I went
to pay my devotions to her shrine. Lucca
drowsed in a haze, her bleached arcades of
trees lifeless in the glare of high noon ; all
the valley was winking, the very bells had
no strength to chime: and then I saw
Ilaria lie in the deep shade waiting for the
judgment. Ilaria was a tall Tuscan—the
girls of Lucca are out of the common tall,
and straight as larches—of fine birth and a
life of minstrels and gardens. Pompous
processions, trapped horses, emblazonings,
were hers, and all refinements of High
Masses and Cardinals. So she lived once a
life as stately-ordered as old dance-music,
in the airy corridors of a great marble

palace, swept hourly by the thin, clear air
of the Lucchesan plain; and her lord went
out to war with Pisa or Pescia, or even
farther afield, following Emperor or Pope
to that Monteaperti which made Arbia run
colour of wine, or shrill Benevento, or
Altopascio which cost the Florentines so
dear.* But Ilaria stayed at home to trifle
with lap-dogs and jongleurs under the
orange trees ; heard boys make stammer-
ing love, and laughed lightly at their
Decameron travesty, being too proud to be
ashamed or angered ; and sometimes (for
she was not too proud but that love should
be of the party), she pulled a ring from
one lithe finger, and looked down while
the lad kissed it for a holy relic and put it
in his bosom reverently,—pretending not
to see. But, Ilaria, you knew well what
gave colour to the faint and worn old words
about *Fior di spin giallo,* or *O Dea fatale,*
or

> " O Dio de' Dei !
> La più bellina mi parete voi ;
> O quanto sete cara agli occhi miei! "

And so the days passed in your square

* Historically he could have done none of these
things, except, perhaps, fight at Altopascio.

corner palace, until the plague came down with the North wind, and you bowed your proud neck before it like a mountain pine. Young to die, young to die and leave the pleasant ways of Lucca, the green ramparts, the grassy walks in the pastures where the hawks fly and the shadows fleet over the green and gold of early May. Young enough, Ilaria. Scorner of love, now Death is at hand, with the bats' wings and wet scythe they give him in the Piazza, when your lord comes triumphing or God's Body takes the air: what of him, Madonna? Let him come, says Ilaria, with raised eyebrows and a wintry smile. Yet she fought: her thin hands held off the scythe at arms' length; she set her teeth and battled with the winged beast. Whenas she knew it must be, suddenly she relaxed her hold, and Death had his way with her.

Then her women came about her and robed her in a long robe, colour of olive leaves, and soft to the touch. And they covered soberly her feet and placed them on a crouching dog, which was Lucca. But her fine hands they folded peace-wise below her bosom, to rest quietly there like the clasps of a girdle. Her gentle hair

(bright brown it was, like a yearling chestnut) they crowned also, and closed down
her ringed eyes. So they let her lie till
judgment come. And when I saw her the
close robe still folded her about and ran
up her throat lovingly to her chin, till her
head seemed to thrust from it as a flower
from its calyx. It would seem, too, as
if her bosom rose and fell, that her nos-
trils quivered when the wind blew in and
touched them; and the hem of her garment being near me, I was fain to kiss
it and say a prayer to the divinity haunting
that place. So I left the presence well disposed in my heart to glorify God for so fair
a sight.

Whereafter I took the way to Florence
among the vineyards and tangled hill-sides;
and, anon, in the broad plain I stayed at
Prato to honour the lady of the town.
Madonna della Cintola she is called now,
and one Luca, a worker in clay, knew her
mind most intimately and did all her will.
Quiet days she had lived at Prato, being
wife to a decent metal-worker there and
keeper of his house and stuff. Mariota she
was then called for all her name; but as
to her parentage none knew it, save that

Marco's Vanna had been both frail and fair, and when she had been in flower the great Lord Ottoboni had flowered likewise—and often in her company. Giovanna I had never known ; she died before her lord married the Lady Adhelidis of Verona and the seven days' tilting were held in her honour in a field below the city wall. But when Luca first knew Mariota and saw how her mother's pride beaconed from her smooth brow, the girl was standing in the Piazza in a tattered green kirtle and bodice that gaped at the hooks, played upon by sun, and fallow wind, and longing looks driven at her eyes in vain. The wench carried her head and light fardel of years like a Princess; would laugh to show her fine teeth if your jest pleased her; and then she would look straightly upon you and be glad of you. If you pleased her not, she would look through you to the mountains or the church-tower. She had as squarely a modelled chin as ever I saw, and her lips firmly set and redder than strawberries in a wet May. None taught her anything; none, that Luca could learn, gave her sup or bed. He was a boy then and would have given her both. I think she knew he favoured her—what girl does not ? Everybody favoured Mariota,—stayed as she passed, and followed her stealthily with troubled eyes. But he was a moody boy then, at the mercy of dreams, and stammered when he was near her, blushing. When he came back she was seventeen years old, and the metal-worker's wife. It was then Luca saw her, in the street called of the Eye, where climbing plants top the convent wall and from the garden comes the scent of wall-flowers and sweet marjoram.

At her man's door she was standing, barefooted, fray - kirtled as of old ; but riper, of more assured and triumphant beauty. In her arms a boy-child, lusty and half-naked, struggled to be fed, seeking with both fat hands to forage for himself. Turning her grey eyes, where pride slumbered and shame had never been, she knew Luca again, made him welcome at the door, with superb assurance set wine and olives and bread before him; and so stood at the table while he ate, gravely recovering one by one the features of his face, smiling, preoccupied with her pleasure and unconscious of the cooing child. For with

matronly composure she had eased my
gentleman as soon as she had provided for
her guest.

In comes the metal-worker, Sor Matteo,
burly but watchful in a greasy apron, eyes
the lad up and down with much burden-
some pondering of hand to scrubby chin,
as to say to Mariota "I'm no fool." With
never a blush, nor a quailing of the eyes'
level beam, Mariota begs cousin Luca to
become conscious of her master.

There were the makings of a piece of
right Boccacesque in all this, and the *pa-
drone* showed manifest disinclination for
his accustomed part: but Luca's candid
face disclaimed all dark-entry work. Mariota hurried to her task. A modeller in
clay, a statuary, *via,* an admirer of the
choicer contrivings of Mother Nature! What
and if he should find his cousin, his scarce-
remembered gossip Mariota, worth an artist's half - closed eye ! And the *bambin-
accio* (with a side-look and face averted
as she spoke)—*ecco!*—many a Gesulino
showed a leaner thigh and cheeks less
peachy than he. Had Papa seen the new
dimple in Beppino's chin? And more soft
piping to the same tune. Master Matteo

was appeased; but Luca was far adrift with other matters. Love, for him, lay not in flesh and blood alone; rather, in what flesh and blood signified in another clay, not Messer Domeneddio's, but his own chosen task-stuff. He had come hither to Prato on the commission of the Opera, to work a *Madonna col Bambino* for the great door of the Duomo. Well! he had his Madonna to hand, it would seem: — Mariota at the door of the smith's house, confident, lissom and fresh, and the lusty child groping for his breakfast. The light had been upon her, gleamed upon her skin, her brimming eyes, her glossy brown hair. What a bravery was hers! What a glorified presentment of young life, new-budded, was here! The town gaped, the husband admired ; but Mariota, with her square chin and high carriage, looked as straightly before her, when in pale blue and silver-white, Madonna with the Babe and the holy deacons Stephen and Laurence stood, four months afterwards, within the shadow of the great church, and shone out to the day.

I pay silent respect to strapping Mariota and her baby-boy in the country of Boccace.

Then, when I am in Florence again, under the spell of the city life, I lounge in the Borg' Ognissanti, or across Arno in the *quartiere* San Niccolò, or out by San Frediano where Botticelli in his green old age pruned his vines, or in the pent streets between the Via della Pergola and Santa Croce, and watch the townsfolk lead their lives of patchwork and easy laughter. I fear I have a taste for such company. I am fond of verdure; I like trees as well as men: every oak for me has its hamadryad informing it. I like flowers better than men; and the most beautiful flower I know is a

girl. I have a sweetheart in the Bargello, as
you shall hear. I believe she is one of Donatello's sowing ; but the critics are divided.
I cannot trace Verocchio's bluntened linea-
ments in her, nor Mino's peaksomeness,
nor anything of Desiderio. She's not very
pretty, but she's like a summer flower,
say, a campanula ; and that is why I love
to watch her and talk to her in this grand-
fatherly fashion. Bettina, I say to her, are
you, I wonder, twelve years old yet? You
cannot be much more I think, for you have
let your bodice-strap slip off one of your
shoulders and betray you to the sun. You
are but a round rosebud now and no one
thinks any harm ; but some day the sun
will look at you in an odd way, and then,
suddenly, you will be ashamed, and draw
your frock right up to your neck.

And your hair strays where it likes at
present. I know you have a golden fillet
of box-leaves round your brow: that is
because you are only a little girl still, not
more than twelve. And you have tied the
ends up in a sort of knot. But you romp
so much and laugh so—I know you have
two bright rows of little teeth—that you
can never expect to keep tidy. Why,

even now, while I am scolding you, you are itching to laugh and run away. I see a wavy lock trailing down your neck, *ragazza*, and those heavy tresses on your temples, instead of being drawn meekly back, droop down over your temples, and cover up your little ears. Don't you know that Florentine ladies are proud of their foreheads, and when they have pretty ears always show them ? Some day, my dear, you will go out into the world ; and your hair will be twisted up into coils with gold braid; perhaps you will have on it a flowery garland of Messer Domenico's making, and a string of Venice beads round your throat. And when the time comes, you won't let the sun play with your neck any more ; he won't know his romp when he sees her in stiff velvet of Genoa and a high collar edged with seed-pearls.

And you won't look me in the eyes as you are doing now, saucy girl, with your chin pushed forward and your mouth all in a pucker—who 's to know whether you are going to pout or giggle ?—and your pert green eyes wide open, as if to say " Who 's this old thickhead staring at me so hard ? " No, Bettina, you will drop them instead ;

you will blush all over your neck and cheeks, and hang your round head. You have chestnuts in your two fists now I know; there's some of the flour sticking to the corners of your mouth, little slut. But then you will have a fan perhaps, or a spy-glass, or at least a mass-book in the mornings; and when I am looking at you, your fingers will tie themselves in knots and be very interesting. In two years' time, Bettina!

But though I sha'n't love you half as much as I do now, I shall always come to see you I think; and, as I shall be a very old man by that time, perhaps you will still sit on a stool at my knee and give me a kiss now and then — oh, a mere bird's peck, just for kindness. . . . The Via de' Bardi is grey, and you are there in yellow. You are like a young daffodil dancing in the winter grass. But soon you will have strained to your full flower-time, and I see you in your summering, lithe and rather languid, with heavy-lidded eyes, and a slow smile. Then you will not dance; but, instead, you will stoop gravely like a tall garden lily, and give your white hand to the lover kneeling below.

And all in two years, my little Bettina!

X

CATS

THERE was once a man in Italy—so the
story runs—who said that animals
were sacred because God had made them.
People did n't believe him for a long time ;
they came, you see, of a race which had
found it amusing to kill such things, and
killed a great many of them too, until it
struck them one fine day that killing men
was better sport still, and watching men
kill each other the best sport of all because
it was the least trouble. Animals ! said
they, why, how can they be sacred ; things
that you call beef and mutton when they
have left off being oxen and sheep, and
sell for so much a pound ? They scoffed at
this mad neighbour, looked at each other
waggishly and shrugged their shoulders as
he passed along the street. Well ! then,
all of a sudden, as you may say, one morning he walked into the town—Gubbio it
was—with a wolf pacing at his heels—a
certain wolf which had been the terror of

the country-side and eaten I don't know how many children and goats. He walked up the main street till he got to the open Piazza in front of the great church. And the long grey wolf padded beside him with a limp tongue lolling out between the ragged palings which stood him for teeth. In the middle of the Piazza was a fountain, and above the fountain a tall stone crucifix. Our friend mounted the steps of the cross in the alert way he had (like a little bird, the story says), and the wolf, after lapping apologetically in the basin, followed him up three steps at a time. Then with one arm round the shaft to steady himself, he made a fine sermon to the neighbours crowding in the Square, and the wolf stood with his fore-paws on the edge of the fountain and helped him. The sermon was all about wolves (naturally) and the best way of treating them. I fancy the people came to agree with it in time; any-how when the man died they made a saint of him and built three churches, one over another, to contain his body. And I believe it is entirely his fault that there are a hun-dred-and-three cats in the convent-garden of San Lorenzo in Florence. For what are

SAN LORENZO

you to do ? Animals are sacred, says Saint
Francis. Animals are sacred, but cats have
kittens ; and so it comes about that the
people who agree with Saint Francis have
to suffer for the people who don't.

The Canons of San Lorenzo agree with
Saint Francis, and it seems to me that they
must suffer a good deal. The convent is
large ; it has a great mildewed cloister
with a covered-in walk all round it built
on arches. In the middle is a green garth
with cypresses and yews dotted about ;
and when you look up you see the blue
sky cut square, and the hot tiles of a huge
dome staring up into it. Round the cloister
walk are discreet brown doors, and by the
side of each door a brass plate tells you
the name and titles of the Canon who lives
behind it. It is on the principle of Dean's
Yard at Westminster ; only here there are
more Canons—and more cats.

The Canons live under the cloister; the
cats live on the green garth, and sometimes
die there. I did not see much of the Canons; but the cats seemed to me very sad—
depressed, nostalgic even, might describe
them, if there had not been something
more languid, something faded and spiritless

about their habit. It was not that they quarrelled. I heard none of those long-drawn wails, gloomy yet mellow soliloquies, with which our cats usher in the crescent moon or hymn her when she swims at the full: there lacked even that comely resignation we may see on any sunny window - ledge at home ; — the rounded back and neatly ordered tail, the immaculate fore-paws peering sedately below the snowy chest, the squeezed-up eyes which so resolutely shut off a bleak and (so to say) unenlightened world. That is pensiveness, sedate, chastened melancholy; but it is soothing, it speaks a philosophy, and a certain balancing of pleasures and pains. In San Lorenzo cloister, when I looked in one hot noon seeking a refuge from the glare and white dust of the city, I was conscious of a something sinister that forbade such an even existence for the smoothest - tempered cat. There were too many of them for companionship and perhaps too few for the humour of the thing to strike them: in and out the chilly shades they stalked gloomily, hither and thither, like lank and unquiet ghosts of starved cats. They were of all colours—

gay orange-tawny, tortoiseshell with the
becoming white patch over one eye, delicate tints of grey and fawn and lavender,
brindle, glossy sable; and yet the gloom
and dampness of the place seemed to mil-
dew them all so that their brightness was
glaring and their softest gradations took on
a shade as of rusty mourning. No cat
could be expected to do herself justice.

To and fro they paced, balancing sometimes with hysterical precision on the ledge
of the parapet, passing each other at whis-
ker's length, but *cutting each other dead!*
Not a cat had a look or a sniff for his
fellow; not a cat so much as guessed at another's existence. Among those hundred-
and-three restless spirits there was not a
cat but did not affect to believe that a
hundred-and-two were away! It was
horrible, the *inhumanity* of it. Here were
these shreds and waifs, these "unnecessary
litters" of Florentine households, herded together in the only asylum (short of the Arno)
open to them, driven in like dead leaves
in November, flitting dismally round and
round for a span, and watching each other
die without a mew or a lick! Saint Francis
was not the wise man I had thought him.

It was about two o'clock in the afternoon. I had watched these beasts at their feverish exercises for nearly an hour before I perceived that they were gradually hemming me in. They seemed to be forming up, in ranks, on the garth. Only a ditch separated us—I was in the cloister-walk, a hundred-and-three gaunt, expectant, desperate cats facing me. Their famished pale eyes pierced me through and through; and two-hundred-and-two hungry eyes (four cats supported life in one apiece) is more than I can stand, though I am a married man with a family. These brutes thought I was going to feed them! I was preparing weakly for flight when I heard steps in the gateway; a woman came in with a black bag. She must be going to deposit a cat on Jean-Jacques' ingenious plan of avoiding domestic trouble; it was surely impossible she wanted to borrow one ! Neither: she came confidently in, beaming on our mad fellowship with a pleasant smile of preparation. The cats knew her better than I did. Their suspense was really shocking to witness. While she was rolling her sleeves up and tying on her apron—she was poor, evidently, but very neat and wholesome in her black dress and the decent cáp which crowned her grey hair—while she unpacked the contents of the bag—two newspaper parcels full of rather distressing viands, scissors, and a pair of gloves which had done duty more than once—while all these preparations were soberly fulfilling, the agitation of the hundred-and-three was desperate indeed. The air grew thick, it quivered with the lashing of tails; hoarse mews echoed along the stone walls, paws were raised and let fall with the rhythmical patter of raindrops. A furtive beast played the thief: he was one of the one-eyed fraternity, red with mange. Somehow he slipped in between us; we discovered him crouched by the newspaper raking over the contents. This was no time for ceremony; he got a prompt cuff over the head and slunk away shivering and shaking his ears. And then the distribution began. Now, your cat, at the best of times, is squeamish about his food; he stands no tricks. He is a slow eater, though he can secure his dinner with the best of us. A vicious snatch, like a snake, and he has it. Then he spreads himself out to dispose of the prey—feet tucked well in, head low, tail laid close along, eyes shut fast. That is how a cat of breeding loves to dine. Alas ! many a day of intolerable prowling, many a black vigil, had taken the polish off the hundred-and-three. As a matter of fact they behaved abominably: they leaped at the scraps, they clawed at them in the air, they bolted them whole with starting eyes and portentous gulpings, they growled all the while with the smothered ferocity of thunder in the hills. No waiting of turns, no licking of lips and moustaches to get the lingering flavours, no dalliance. They were as restless and suspicious here as everywhere; their feast was the horrid hasty orgy of ghouls in a churchyard.

But an even distribution was made: I don't think any one got more than his share. Of course there were underhand attempts in plenty and, at least once, open violence—a sudden rush from opposite sides, a growling and spitting like sparks from a smithy; and then, with ears laid flat, two ill-favoured beasts clawed blindly at each other, and a sly and tigerish brindle made away with the morsel. My woman took the thing very coolly I thought, served them all alike, and did n't resent (as I should have done) the unfortunate want of delicacy there was about these vagrants. A cat that takes your food and growls at you for the favour, a cat that would eat *you* if he dared, is a pretty revelation. *Ça donne furieusement à penser.* It gives you a suspicion of just how far the polish we most of us smirk over will go. My cats at San Lorenzo knew some few moments of peace between two and three in the afternoon. That would have been the time to get up a testimonial to the kind soul who fed them. Try them at five and they would ignore you. But try them next morning !

My knowledge of the Italian tongue, in those days, was severely limited to the necessaries of existence ; to try me on a fancy subject, like cats, was to strike me dumb. But at this stage of our intercourse (hitherto confined to smiles and eye-service) it became so evident my companion had something to say that I must perforce take my hat off and stand attentive. She pointed to the middle of the garth, and there, under the boughs of a shrub, I saw the hundred-and-fourth cat, sorriest of them all. It was a new-comer, she told me, and shy. Shy it certainly was, poor wretch ; it glowered upon me from under the branches like a bad conscience. Shyness could not hide hunger—I never saw hungrier eyes than hers—but it could hold it in check: the silkiest speech could not tempt her out, and when we threw pieces she only winced ! What was to be done next was my work. Plain duty called me to scale the ditch with some of those dripping, slippery, nameless cates in my fingers and to approach the stranger where she lurked bodeful under her tree. My passage towards her lay over the rank vegetation of the garth, in whose coarse herbage here and there I stumbled upon a limp white form stretched out—a waif the less in the world ! I don't say it was a happy passage for me : it was made to the visible consternation of her I wished to befriend. Her piteous yellow eyes searched mine for sympathy ; she wanted to tell me something and I would n't understand ! As I neared her she shivered and mewed twice. Then she limped painfully off—poor soul, she had but three feet !— to another tree, leaving behind her, unwillingly enough, a much-licked dead kitten. That was what she wanted to tell me then. As I was there, I deposited the garbage by the side of the little corpse, knowing she would resume her watch, and retired. My friend who had put up her parcels was prepared to go. She thanked me with a smile as she went out, looking carefully round lest she had missed out some other night-birds.

One of the Canons had come out of his door and was leaning against the lintel, thoughtfully rubbing his chin. He was a spare dry man who seemed to have measured life and found it a childish business. He jerked his head towards the gateway as he glanced at me. "That is a good woman," he said in French, "she lendeth unto the Lord. . . . Yes," he went on, nodding his head slowly backwards and forwards, "lends Him something every day." The cats were sitting in the shady cloister-garth licking their whiskers : one was actually cleaning his paw. I went out into the sun thinking of Saint Francis and his wolf.

XI

THE SOUL OF A CITY

HE hated Marco first of all because one day he undersold him in the Campo, put him to shame in open market. Figs were going cheap that October in spite of the waning year ; but there was no earthly reason why he should give the English ladies more than four for two *soldi*. What were *soldi* to English people ? The scratch of a flea ! He would have given them a handful, taken as they came, for their piece of *cinquanta,* and reaped a tidy little profit for himself. Who would have been the worse ? God knew he needed it. Mariola crumpled with the ague like a dried leaf, and that long girl of his growing up so fast, and still running wild with goat-herds and marble quarrymen. How could he send her to the nuns for a place unless he bought her some shoes and a rosary ? And then that pig Marco—thieving old miser—peered forward with his mock candour and silver-rimmed goggles and offered *ten* for two *soldi*—ten ! with the market price, *Dio mio,* at twelve ! And *fichi totati* too ! Do you wonder that the ladies in striped blankets gave the cheek to Maso Cecci and turned to Marco Zoppa ?

That was n't all, but it was an accentuation of a long series of spiteful injuries wrought him by the wrinkled old villain. Maso endured, hating the old man daily more and more ; tried little tricks, little revenges, upon him, upset his baskets, hid his pipe ; but they generally failed or recoiled with a nasty swiftness upon himself. He only got deeper and deeper into the bad odour of the neighbours who traded in the Piazza with fruit and indifferent photographs. Nothing went very well— thanks to that unspeakable old Marco! His girl grew longer and lazier and handsomer, with a shapelier bust and a pair of arms like that snaky Bacchante in the *Opera.* Maso had to quail more than he liked to admit before the proud stare of her eyes; and when she dropped the heavy lids upon them and sauntered away, arms akimbo under her shawl, he could only swear. And he always cursed Marco Zoppa, who gave her chestnuts and sage counsel for nothing. God only knew what devilry he might be whispering to her in the shady corner where the sun never came and the grass sprouted between the flags—she leaning against the wall, looking down at her toes, and he peering keen-eyed into her face and muttering in his beard, sometimes laying an old brown hand on her shoulder —Lord! he *did* hate the man.

Then came the August races.

Maso had brought his Isotta into the city to see the fun and she had disappeared in the press just before the procession stayed by the Palazzo and the trumpets sounded for the first race. Maso shrugged his shoulders and cursed his luck, but did n't budge. The girl must look after herself. He was on the upper rim of the great fountain craning his neck over the pack of people: then he got a dig under the ribs enough to take the breath of an ox. It was the spout of old Marco's green umbrella. "Hey! silly fool," spluttered the old liar, "dost want that loose-legged slut of thine in trouble? I tell thee she 's playing in a corner with Carlo Formaggia. Already he 's pinched her cheek twice, and who knows what the end may be? Mud-coloured ass, wilt thou let they child slip to the devil while thou standest gaping at a horse-race?" And this before all the neighbours! What to say to such a man? Maso babbled with rage; but he had to go, for Carlo Formaggia was well known. He had ruined more girls than enough; he was in league with vile houses, gambling dens, thieves' hells; Captain of an infamous secret society; the police were only waiting for a pretext to get him shipped off to the hulks. He must go of course. No thanks to Marco though: in fact he hated him worse than ever, partly because he had drawn all eyes and a fair share of sniggering and tongues thrust in the cheek upon his account; but most because he knew he had been trapped into losing a good place. For, as he mounted the narrow stair cut between old houses steep as rocks, he turned and saw Zoppa placidly smoking his pipe in the very spot he had held, squatted on the fountain-rim with his green umbrella between his knees. He was beaming through his spectacles, in a fatherly, indulgent sort of way, upon the shouting people; following the race too, like one who had paid for his box. Maso, when

he heard the shatter of hoofs and the wild
roar from thousands of throats down below
him in the Campo, cursed old Zoppa with a
grey face, and went muttering round the
blinding sides of the Duomo to find his
daughter. And when he did find her she
was eating chestnuts at the open door of her
aunt's shop in the Via Ghibellina ! Bacchus!
she was sick of all those folk in their *festa*
clothes, was all the explanation she would
give him from between fine white teeth all
clogged with chestnut-meal. If he chose
to dress his daughter like a beggar's brat
he had better not take her to the races.
Maso's feeling of relief at finding her alone
and looking her usual sulky impassive self
gave way very rapidly to a sort of right-
eous wrath against his triumphant enemy.
So, by foul slanders of honest, God-fearing
people that old Jew had not scrupled to
rob him of his place ! His place and his
day's fun. By Heaven, he was tricked,
duped by a scaly-eyed Jew pedlar, a vile
old dog tottering down to Hell with lies in
his beard. Well ! he would put this
morning's work down to his score ; some
day there would be a choice little reckoning
for Ser Marco.

184

Maso, green with impotent fury, poured
out his flood of gutturals upon his *insouci-
ante* child. General reproaches were always
a failure in cases of this sort. Some were
sure to be wild guess-work and to drown
the real ones : you could never tell when
you had hit the mark. Had she not—she
fourteen, too !—slid astride down the rail-
ing into the Campo and been caught up in
the arms of Carlo Formaggia waiting and
laughing at the bottom ? Had she not lain
a whole minute in his arms, panting ?
And then, *Dio mio,* with the sweat still on
her forehead, she had slipped off to San
Domenico and confessed to coughing at
mass the Sunday before ! Pest ! he would
give her the strap over her shoulders when
he got her home. The long, brown girl
leaned against the lintel kicking one heel
idly against the other. She was smiling at
him, smiling with her lazy, languid eyes
and with her glistening teeth. Every now
and then she inspected a chestnut critically
—like an amateur !—and slipped it between
her jaws. They split it like a banana.
And then she squeezed the half skins and
dropped the flour down her throat. She
had a long sinewy throat, glossy as velvet,

with its silvery lights and dusky brown shadows. Maso stood helpless before her as she drank down her flour ; he chattered like a little passionate ape. At last he lifted up both hands in a sudden frenzy of despair and went away.

Of course the races were over. The sober streets swarmed with people in their holiday clothes. They all seemed laughing and smoking, and talking fluently of something ridiculous. Maso, egoist, knew it must be about him—or his daughter. Arms and heads went like mill-sails or tall trees in a gale of wind. Then, with a rattle and the sudden sliding of four hoofs on the flags, a cart would be in the thick of them, and the people scoured to the curb, still laughing, or spitting between the spasms of the interrupted jest. The boys tried to peep under the sagging hats of the girls, and the girls turned pettish shoulders to them and, as they turned, you caught the glint of fun in their great roes' eyes and saw the lips part before the quick breath. The streets were mere gullies, clefts hewn in zig-zag between grey houses that tottered up and up, and lay over them like cliffs. An ancient church with bleached

stone saints under flowery canopies, a
guttering candle before a tinsel shrine, and
the hoarse babel of the streets—whips that
cracked and spluttered like squibs, a swarm-
ing coloured stream of men and maids, once
the twang of a chance mandoline.   Siena
was feasting, and the waiters furtively
swept their foreheads with their coatsleeves
as they ran in and out of the *trattorie*.

In the *trattoria* of the *Aquila Rossa* old
Marco Zoppa smoked his pipe and talked,
between the spurts of smoke, to his neighbours.   Fate brought him face to face with
two enemies at once.   Maso was battling
his way up the street, white and strained
as a grave-cloth ; and Carlo Formaggia,
the approved bravo—oiled and jaunty, with
his brown felt fantastically rolled and stuck
over one ear, with a long cigar which he
alternately gnawed and sucked, Carlo the
broad-chested, of the seared, evil face,
came down with the stream on the arms
of two other gilded youths.   They met
before the café, the man of intolerable
wrongs and the Pilia-Borsa of Siena.   Maso
scowled till his thick eyebrows cut his face
horizontally in two.   He stood ostenta-
tiously still, muttering with his lips as the

trio went lightly by. Then he made to go on. But old Marco Zoppa stood up and made a speech. He had the wooden stem of his pipe 'twixt finger and thumb, and used it like a conductor's *bâton* to emphasise his points. As his voice shrilled and quavered, Carlo Formaggia caught his own name and turned back to listen, prickeared. He stood out of sight resting one foot on a doorstep, and leaned forward on to his leg. He might have been dreaming of some night of love, but he held every word as it dropped.

" Maso," Marco went on, "thou art but a thin fool. I know what I know ; but thou must needs stick dirt in thine ears and pass me by. Well, let be, let be ; the end will come soon enough—this night even. And I have warned thee."

"Spawn of a pig, wilt never have done irking me? See, I scratch thee off me !" Maso drove home his gibe with a dramatic performance. The *trattoria* was agape. Every table held its three craning necks and six piercing, twinkling eyes atop.

" I grow old, my Maso, I grow very old, and thy monkey's tricks are nought. 'T is thy slip of a girl and thy poor twisted

Mariola I would save in spite of thee.
Listen then once more, and for the last
time. Ser Carlo intends to snare thy
pigeon. He has limed his twigs ; the bird
flutters free for this noon, but by to-
night she will be caged. For me, I have
done my possible—but I am old. Life
tingles fiercer in the blood of a young
man. Therefore beware. Wilt thou see
that brawny assassin toying with thy girl ;
leaning over her where she crouches, poi-
soning her with fat words? That's how
the snake licks the turtle before he gulps
her—'t is to make her sleek, look you !
Well, go thy way, dolt and blunderhead.
For me—old as I am—I will shoot a last
bolt for Mariola. This very night after
supper I go to the Sbirro : and thy thanks
will be a rounder oath and some more
knave's tricks with my baskets."

"No thanks are owing, Marco Zoppa";
Maso was ashy with shame and rage at the
old man's placid benevolence. "Marco
Zoppa, thou hast been my enemy ever, and
I have borne it "—the Café roared with
laughter; a fat old Capuchin nearly had a
fit. Maso looked round with fright in his
eyes. He went on, "Now thou hast

gone too far—insulting me grossly before
these citizens. Thou hast brought thine
end upon thyself." He ran away fighting
through the delighted crowd. Everybody
who could get at him slapped him on the
back. A big carter stove his hat in.

Old Marco shrugged his patient shoulders and sat down to read the *Secolo*. He
balanced his silver-rimmed spectacles on
his nose and held the journal at arm's
length with hand a thought more shaky,
perhaps, than usual. Presently he looked
up: "Mother of God! what a white-faced
rogue it is! Eh, Giuseppe?" "By Mars,
if looks could stab, thou hadst been riddled
by the knife before this," said his friend.
Marco shrugged and went on reading—he
was an old man.

But when Carlo Formaggia had heard
the debate, he turned a shade shinier, and
his eyes harder and brighter. As he motioned his friends off with a look, he swallowed something hard in his throat. Then
he turned down the first side street,
doubled round to the right, turned to the
left down a kind of black sewer-trap and
let himself into a wine-shop where he sat
down, breathing short. He drank brandy

—but he drank like a machine. The muscles of his jaw were working spasmodically as he sat rigid on a tub, leaning against the counter. And he fingered something at his belt. His eyes were in a cold stare: he saw nothing and did n't move. But he went on drinking brandy till late in the afternoon, till the *Hail Mary* bells began to sound a tinkling chorus through the still air.

And Maso Cecci, he too, rushed away white and chattering. Rage had past definition with him, he saw things red, and they choked him. The air felt thick to him, full of flies. He brushed his hands before his face, struck out vaguely, and swore as the dazzling black things settled round him again in a swarm. Irritated, maddened as he was, he still heard the derisive yells of the crowd at the *birreria* and saw Marco's calm wise old face smiling urbanely behind silver spectacles. *Cristo amore!* how he loathed that old man. Siena could never hold the pair of them : there must be an end—there *should* be an end. His heart gave a jerk under his vest as he thought of it. An end !—an end of his eternal fretting jealousy in the Campo, his continued sense of being worsted, of galling inferiority to that methodical old villain. An end of his worries about Isotta; an end—ah! but there would be something rarer than that? To a man like Maso, a small man, of immoderate self-esteem, and that self-esteem always on the smart, there is another satisfaction—that of seeing the better man totter and slip forward to his knees. This insufferable old Marco who was always so right, with his slow methods and accursed accuracy—to see him stumble and drop! That was what made Maso's heart flutter and thud against his skin. And then, as he thought of it, it seemed inevitable. It could be done in a minute, *via!* The old man was alone—it would be dusk —he would peer forward through the gloom to open the door and—*Madre di Dio!*—and then! Maso was sweating; the back of his palate itched intolerably; something hot and sticky clogged his mouth and glued his tongue against the roof of it. His knees shook so that he could scarcely walk. Some little boys stood to stare at him as he lurched by, and laughed stealthily to see the hated Maso tipsy. But Maso was unconscious of all this: he staggered on homewards with scorching eyes. . . .

Old Marco lived down beyond the Railway Station—a room in a crazy block of buildings that had been run up for the needs of the factory hands. It was like a great smooth cliff, this block, and was washed over a raw pink, but it glowed in the setting sun that evening, like the city herself and all the hills, the colour of bright blood. As Maso neared its blind face, stepping warily with outstretched neck like some obscene bird, and with one hand under his coat—the sun was going down into a purple bank of cloud. He gilded the edges as he sank and shot broad rays of crimson light up into the green sky. Here and there a star twinkled faint ; the city lay over him like a cloudy, silent company of rocks ; the tower of the Palazzo ran up into the pallor of the sky, a shaking spear.

There was but one glimmer of light in the whole ghostly wall of tenements and that, Maso knew, was Marco Zoppa's. Every soul else was crowded in the Campo waiting for the fireworks. And, as he thought, he heard a dull thud behind him, and turned ; and there, far up, a single shaft of flame shot aloft, and stayed, and burst into a fan of lights ; and a puff told him it was the first rocket. *"Ecco! Madre di Dio,* a sign! a sign! So will *I* go up ; and so shall my enemy come down." And Maso crept up the stairway breathing thick and short. . . .

With a hand still under his cloak he rapped his knuckles on the door. No answer. An echo, only, fluttered and grew faint down the stone steps. He hoisted his cloak from the shoulder and swung his right arm free. Then he knocked again. Nothing. No sign. Heavy silence ; only a distant murmur of voices, muffled and infinitely far, from the Campo on the hill.

"The game has flown ! Or the old dog sleeps." Maso sighed, for he wanted to see him drop gurgling to his knees. Still, it made his affair easier. He gave one fierce hoist to his cloak, twitched his right arm once or twice, and gently turned the handle. Then he stepped lightly and daintily into the room.

A candle guttered on a little table in the corner, and the Crucified showed white upon the black cross above. Marco Zoppa lay on his bed with his throat cut from ear to ear. The cut was so resolute that his head stuck out at an angle from his body—almost a right angle ; and in some struggle he had got his nostril sliced. That gave him an odd, *mesquin* expression, lying there with his mouth open and his yawning nostril, as if he wanted to sneeze. The room smelt stale and sour ; the thick air gathered in a misty halo round the candle, and a fat shroud of tallow drooped over the edges of the candlestick.

Maso dropped his long, clean knife ; dropped on to his knees and wailed like a chained dog. He could not take his eyes from the horrible black pit between the dead man's chin and trunk. Out of that pit a thin scarlet stream was still slipping lazily, and crawling down the white coverlet to the floor. Maso's wailing attracted a dog near by. He too set off howling from behind his door : and then another, and another. There was a chorus of howls, long-drawn, pitiful, desolate ; and Maso, the only man in that woeful company, howled like any dog of the pack.

Gradually his moaning sank and then stopped with a dry sob. He crawled on his knees a little nearer to the bed and eyed fearfully a patch of blood on the counterpane. Just God! what was that patch? A faint circle smeared with the finger, and through the midst of it a ragged dart. Carlo Formaggia had been there! He knew that mark! And then the whole truth blazed before him like a sheet of fire. He fell forward on his face. The thin thread of scarlet from Marco Zoppa's gaping throat crawled drop by drop on to his shoulder.

Carlo Formaggia had limed his bird.

XII

WITH THE BROWN BEAR

THE secret of happy travelling is contrast. Suffer, that you may drowse thereafter : grill, that you may have a heat on you worth assuagement. Wherefore, to the Italian wanderer, it will be worth while to endure the fierceness of the Lombard plain, even the gilded modernisms of Milan (blistering though they may be under the stroke of the naked sun) and the dusty, painful traverse of the Apennines, to drop down at last into the broad green peace of the Val d'Arno. Take, however, the first halting-place you can. You will find yourself in a hollow of the hills, helping the brown bear of Pistoja keep the Northern gates of Tuscany. It is not unlikely that the Apennine may " walk abroad with the storm," or hide his moss-brown slopes in great sheets of mist. This, while it means a fine sight, means also rain for Pistoja. A quiet rain will accordingly fall upon the little city, gently but persistently. Only in the gleams may you guess that you have the Tuscan sky over you and the smiling Tuscan Art round about. But the ways of the Pistolesi will confirm the feeble knees : such at least was my case.

For the Pistolesi were there besides foul weather, and splashed about under green umbrellas with prodigious jokes to cut at each other's expense, of a sort we reserve for Spring or early June. For them, with a vintage none too good to be garnered, it might have been the finest weather in the world ; but I am bound to add my belief that they would have laughed were it the worst. With no money, no weather, and taxes intolerable, Pistoja laughed and looked handsome. Was not Boccaccio a Pistolese ? I was reminded of his book at every turn of the road : life is a wanton story there, or, say, a Masque of Green Things, enacted by a splendid fairy rout. They were still the well-favoured race Dino Compagni described them far back in the fourteenth century—"formati di bella statura oltre a' Toscani," he says. The words hold good of their grandsons—the men leaner and longer, hardier and keener than you find them in Lucca or Siena ; and the

women carry their heads high, and when
they smile at you (as they will) you think
the sun must be shining. They are mount-
aineers, a strong race. At *pallone* one
day, I saw muscles " all a-ripple down the
back," arms, and shoulders, which would
have intoxicated the great old "amatore
del persona" himself. For their vivacity,
it is racial ; I think all Tuscans, more or
less, retain the buoyant spirits, the alertness
as of birds, which crowned Italy with
Florence instead of Rome or Milan. Tuscan Art is a proof of that, and Tuscan Art
can be studied at its roots in Pistoja : you
see there the naked thing itself with none
of the wealth of Florence to make the
head swim. If Florence had stopped
short at the death of Giuliano de' Medici,
you might say Pistoja was Florence seen
through the diminishing-glass. Is not that
ribbed dome, with its purple mass domi-
neering over the huddled roofs, Brunelleschi's ? It is a faithful copy of Vasari's
hatching ; but no matter. So with the
Baptistry, the towers, the grim old cor-
niced palaces, the *sdruccioli* and gloomy
clefts which serve for streets. But you
would be wrong. Pisa is the real parent

of Pistoja, as indeed she is of Florence—
Dante's Florence. Pisa's magnificent building repeats too itself here : Gothic with
a touch of Latin sanity, a touch of the
genuine Paganism which loves the dædal
earth and cannot bring itself to be out of
touch with it. San Giovanni *fuori-civitas*,
what a rock-hewn church it is ! A rigid
oblong, dark as the twilight, running with
the street without belfry or window or
façade. Three tiers of shallow arcades on
spiral columns, never a window to be seen,
and the whole of solemn black marble
narrowly striped with white. Is there
such a beast as a black tiger—a tiger where
the tawny and black change places? San
Giovanni is modelled after that fashion.
It is very old—twelfth century at latest—
very shabby and weather-beaten, dusty
and deserted. But it will outlive Pistoja ;
and that is probably what Pistoja desired.

This black and white, which is so re-
miniscent of early Florence, is carried out
with more fidelity to the model in the
Piazza. The octagonal Baptistry is, no
doubt, a copy of Dante's beloved church ;
but it is much better placed, does not
"shun to be admired" like its beautiful

yellowed sister. The Duomo is of Pisa again, and has a tower, half belfry, half fortress, which once the Podestà seized and held while the plucky little town endured a siege. The Brown Bear stood out long against the Lily. But Lorenzo showed his teeth: and the Wolf prevailed at last. Sculpture apart, the resemblance to Florence stops here. None of her Cinque-cento bravery and little of her earlier and finer Renaissance came this way. But one thing came; one clean breath from "that solemn fifteenth century" did blow to this verge of Tuscan soil, a breath from Luca della Robbia and his men. They may flower more exuberantly in Florence, those broad, blue-eyed platters of theirs ; nowhere is their purpose more explicit, their charm more exquisitely appreciable than here. There is a chance of considering the art on its own merits ; better, you can see it more truly as it was at home, since Florence has caught some little of Haussmannism and is not as Luca left it. So here, perhaps best of all, you may try to plumb the depths of the Della Robbia soul,—through its purity and limpid candour, through its shining, sweetly wholesome homeliness,

down to the crystal sincerity burning recessed in the shrine. It is the fashion to
say of Angelico da Fiesole that his was a
naïveté which amounted to genius : a thin
phrase, which may nevertheless pass to
qualify the inspired miniaturist. The re-
ligiosity of the Della Robbia, while no less
naïve, is really far other. It is not Gothic
at all, nor ascetic, nor mystic. It would
be Latin, were it not blithe enough to be
Greek. It speaks of what is and must be,
and is well content ; not of what should,
or might be, if one could but tear off this
crust. It seems probable that it speaks as
pure a Paganism—just that very Paganism
which Pisan building represents—as has
been seen since the workmen of Tanagra
fashioned their little clay familiars for the
tombs, slim Greek girls in their reedy habit as
they lived, or chattering matrons like those
you read of in Theocritus. Much fine phrasing has been spent upon the effort to analyse
the æsthetics of Della Robbia ware. Its
inexhaustible charm is unquestionable; but
just where does it catch one's breath ? Not
altogether in the clean colouring, like nothing so much as that of a cool, glazed dairy
at home,—"milky-blue," "cream-white,"

GOTHIC AND LATIN

"butter-yellow," "parsley-green," all the dairy names come pat to pen ;—not necessarily in the sheer, April loveliness of form and expression, though that would count for much ; nor, I believe, as Mr. Pater would have us acknowledge, in the evanescent delicacy of each motive and sentiment,—the arresting of a single sigh, a single wave of desire, a single stave of the Magnificat. All this is true, and true only of Luca, and yet the whole charm is not there. Rather, I think, you will find it in the fusing of humble material—the age-old clay of the potter (of the Master-Potter, for that matter)—and fine art, whereby the wayside shrine is linked to the high altar, and *contadino* and Vicar-Apostolic can hail a common ideal. Every lane, every cottage, has its Madonna-shrine here ; lumped in clay or daubed in raw colour, nothing can obliterate the sweet sentiment of these poor weeds of art, these tawdry little appeals to the better part of us. Madonna cries with a bared red heart ; she supports a white Christ ; she stoops suave to enfold a legion of children in her mantle. She is as Tuscan as the brownest of them ; but a Tuscan of the rarest mould, they would

have you to see, of a cleanliness quite un-
approachable, of a benignity wholly divine.
One learns the secret of devotional art best
of all in such ephemeral sanctuaries. And
since Fine Art is the flower of these shabby
roots, Italy only, where Cincinnatus worked
in his garden, can furnish so wonderful a
harmony of opposites. Surely it is the
most democratic country in Europe. I saw

a Colonel the other day, in Bologna, carrying a newspaper parcel. He was in full
uniform. It was the secret of Saint Francis
that he knew how to bridge the gulf on
either side of which we, prisoners in feu-
dal holds, have cried to each other in vain.
It was the secret of the Della Robbia too.
The god shall sink that we may rise to
meet him in the way. Why not? Here

in Pistoja are some precious pieces—a *Visitation* in San Giovanni, a pearly *Madonna Incoronata* on the big door of San Giacopo, concerning which it would be difficult to account to one's self for the added zest given by the mantle of fine dust which has settled down on the pale folds of the drapery and outlined the square blue panels of the background. After all, is it not one more touch of the hedgerow, a symbol of the hedgerow-faith not quite dead in the byways of Italy?

But I know I shall never convey the spontaneity with which Fra Paolino's *Visitation* strikes quick for the heart. The thing is so momentary, a mere quiver of emotion passing from one woman to another. The pair of them have looked in to the deeps. Then the older stumbles forward to her knees, and the girl stoops down to raise her. One guesses the rest. They will be sobbing together in a minute, the girl's face buried in the other's shoulder. All you are to see is just the wistfulness,—"My dear! my dear!" And then the Virgin, full of Grace, but a shy girl in her teens for all that, hides her hot cheeks and cries her little wild heart to quietness. Some of it is in

Albertinelli's fine picture, but not all. All of it—and here's the point—is to be seen in the street among these clear-eyed Tuscan women, just as Fra Paolino (himself of Pistoja) saw it before our time, and then fixed it for ever in blue and white.

And now cross the Piazza and come down the steep incline by the Palazzo Commune, turn to the left, and behold the crown of Pistoja, the Spedale del Ceppo. Everybody knows Luca's masterpiece at Florence, the Foundling Hospital on whose front are some twenty *bambini* in pure white on- blue: babies or flowers, one does not know which. In 1514 the Pistolesi remodelled their own hospital, and called in the successors to Luca's mystery to make it joyful. Andrea, Giovanni, Luca II., and Girolamo came and conjured in turn, and their wall-flowers sprouted from the limewashed sides. I fancy myself out in the patched Piazza del Ceppo as I write, looking again on the pleasant quietness of it all. It is a grey day with thunder smouldering somewhere in the hills, close and heavy. The blind walls about me stare hard in the raw light, but the wards of the hospital are open back and front to the air; it is a rest for the eye to

look into their cool depths within the loggia.
It is a square, very plain, yellow building,
this hospital, unrelieved save for its loggia, its painted frieze of earthenware, and
a rickety cross to denote its pious uses.
Through the wards I can see to the wet
sky again and a gable-end of vivid red and
yellow. A thin black Christ on his cross
stands up against this bright square of distance, pathetic silhouette enough for me;
reminder something sinister, you might
think, for the sick folk inside. But not so;
this is a crucifix, not a *Crucifixion*. This poor
wooden Rood, bowing in the shade, speaks
not of high tragedy, but of the simple annals
of the poor again; not of St. John, but of St.
Luke. I shall be called sentimental; but
with the band of garden colours before me I
can't get away from the streets and alleys. I
am not sure the craftsmen intended I should.
The hospital itself is low and square ; it
is limewashed all over, and has the blind
and beaten aspect of all Italian houses :—
red-purplish tiles running into deep eaves,
jalousied windows, and the loggia. It is
on the face of this that the workers in
baked clay — "lavoro molto utile per la
state," so cool and fresh is it, so redolent

of green pastures and the winds of April—
have moulded the Seven Acts of Pure
Mercy in colours as pure ; blue of morning
sky, grass-green, daffodil-yellow. Once
more, no heroics : here is what the workmen knew and we see. Black and white
frati, not idealised at all, but sleek and
round in the jaw as a monk will get on oil
and *asciutta,* minister to sun-burnt peasants, and ruddy girls as massive in the
waist and stout in the ankle as their sisters
of to-day. Then, of course, there is Allegory,—Allegory of your well-ordered, grav-
itated sort, which takes us no whit farther
from wholesome earth and the men and
women so plainly and happily made of it.
No soaring, no transcendentalism. Carità
is a deep-breasted market-girl nursing two
brown babies, whom I have just seen
sprawling over a gourd in the Campo
Marzio ; Fortezza, Speranza, Fede, I know
them all, bless their sober, good eyes ! in
the fruit-market, or selling newspapers, or
plaiting straws in the Piazza. After this
we slide into religion pure and direct, the
beautiful ridiculous Paganism which has
never left the plain heathen-folk. Wreathed
medallions in the spandrils give us Mary

warned, Mary visited, Mary homing to her Son, Mary crowned·; what would they do without their Bona Dea in Tuscany? She is of them, and yet always a little beyond their grasp. Not too far, however. That means Gothicism. The advantage of the Italian religious ideal is obvious. Art may never leave for long together the good brown earth; and it can serve religion well when it plucks up a type to set, clean as God made it, just a little above our reach, to show whose is "the earth and the fulness thereof."

An example. I leave the white and crumbling Piazza, its old marble well, its beggars, its sick, and its meadow-fresh border of Della Robbia planting, and stray up the Via del Ceppo towards the ramparts. High at a barred window a brown mother with a brown dependent baby smiles down upon my wayfaring. She has fine broad brows and a patient face ; when she smiles, out of mere kindness for my solitary goings, it is pleasant to note the gleam of light on her teeth and lips. I take off my hat, as Luca or Lippo would have done, to "ma cousine la Reine des cieux."

Thus goes life in Pistoja and the rest of the world.

XIII

DEAD CHURCHES AT FOLIGNO

FROM my roof-top, whither I am fled to snatch what cooler airs may drift into this cup of earth, I can see above the straggling tiles of gable and loggia the cupolas and belfries of many churches. I know they are all dead; for I have wound a devious way through the close, inhospitable streets and met them or their ghosts at every corner. The ghost of a dead church is the worst of all disembodied sighs: he wails and chatters at you. Here I have seen churches whose towers were fallen and their tribunes laid bare to the insults of the work-a-day world. There were churches with ugly gashes in them, fresh and smarting still; some had sightless eyes, as of skulls; and there were churches piecemeal and scattered like the splinters of the True Cross. A great foliated arch of travertine would frame a patch of plaster and soiled casement just broad enough for some lolling pair of shoulders and shock-head atop; a sacred emblem, some *Agnus* indefinably venerable, some proud old cognisance of the See, or frayed Byzantine symbol (plaited with infinite art by its former contrivers), such and other consecrated fragments would stuff a hole to keep the wind away from a donkey-stall or *Fabbrica di pasta* in a muddy lane. I met dismantled walls still blushing with the stains of fresco—a saint's robe, the limp burden of the Addolorata ; — I met texts innumerable, shrines fly-ridden and, often as not, mocked with dead flowers. And now, as I see these grey towers and the grand purple line of the hills hemming in the Tiber Valley, I know I am come down to the sated South, to the confines of Umbria, the country of dead churches, and of Rome the metropolis of such deplorable broken toys. This appears to me the disagreeable truth concerning the harbourage of Saint Francis and Saint Bernardine, and of Roberto da Lecce, a man who, if everybody had his rights, would be known as great in his way as either. You will remember that Luther found it out before me. The religious enthusiasm we bring in may serve our

turn while we are here: it will be odd if
any survive for the return ; impossible to
go away as fervid as we come. Other
enthusiasms will fatten ; but the wonderful Gothic adumbration of Christianity was
born in the North and has never been
healthy anywhere else. Gothicism, driven
southward runs speedily to seed ; an
amazing luxuriance, a riot, strange flowers
of heavy shapes and maddening savour ;
and then that worst corruption to follow a
perfection premature. So mediæval Christianity in Umbria is a ruin, but not for
Salvator Rosa ; it has not been suffered a
dignified death. That is the sharpest cut
of all, that the poor bleached skull must be
decked with paper roses.

All this is forced upon me by my last
days in Tuscany, where a lower mean has
secured a serener reign. I had hardly real-
ised the comeliness of its intellectual vigour
without this abrupt contrast. Pistoja, with
its pleasant worship of the wholesome in
common life; Lucca, girdled with the grey
and green of her immemorial planes, and
adorned with the silvery gloss of old marble and stone-cutter's work exquisitely curious; then Prato, dusty little handful of old

brick palaces and black and white towers, where I heard a mass before the high altar but two Sundays ago. All Prato was in church that showery morning, I think. The air was close, even in the depths of the great nave: the fans all about me kept up a continual flicker, like bats' wings, and the men had to use their hats, or handkerchiefs where they had them. To hear the responses rolling about the chapels and echoing round the timbers of the roof you would have said the thunder had come. It was too dark to see Lippi's light-hearted secularities in the choir; one saw them, however, best in the congregation—the same appealing innocence in the grey-eyed women, and the men with the same grave self-possession and the same respectful but deliberate concern with their own affairs which gives you the idea that they are lending themselves to divine service rather out of politeness than from any more intimate motive. Lippi saw this in Prato four centuries ago, and I, after him, saw it all again in a rustic sacrifice which I should find it hard to distinguish from earlier sacrifices in the same spot. And indeed it is informed with precisely the same spirit, an inarticulate reverence for the Dynamic in Nature. How many religions can be reduced to that! In Florence again, what a hardy slip of the old stock still survives! You may see how the worship of Venus Genetrix and Maria Deipara merged in the work of Botticelli and Ghirlandajo, Michael Angelo and Andrea del Sarto; you may see how, if asceticism has never thriven there, there was (and still is) an effort after selection of some sort and a scrupulous respect for the *elegantia quædam* which Alberti held to be almost divine; you may see, at least, a religion which still binds, and which, making no great professions, has grown orderly and surely to respect. Thus from a Tuscany, pagan, kindly, exuberant and desponding by turns, but always ready with that long slow smile you first meet in the Lorenzetti of Siena and afterwards find so tenderly expressed in its different manifestations in the Della Robbia and Botticelli,—a smile where patience and wistfulness struggle together and finally kiss,—I came down to Umbria and a people dying of what M. Huysmans grandiosely calls "our immense fatigue." Here is a people that has loved asceticism not wisely. This asceticism, pushed to the limit where it becomes a kind of sensuality, has bitten into Umbria's heart; and Umbria, with a cloyed palate, sees her frescos peel and lets her sanctuaries out to bats and green lizards. Surely the worst form of moral jaundice is where the sufferer watches his affections palsy, but makes no stir.

From the ramp of the citadel at Perugia you can guess what a hornet's nest that grey stronghold of the Baglioni must have been. It commands the great plain and bars the way to Rome. Westward, on a spur of rock, stands Magione and a lonely tower : this was their outpost towards Siena. Eastward there is a white patch on the distant hills—Spello, "mountain built with quiet citadel," quiet enough now. There was always a Baglione at Spello with his eyes set on chance comers from Foligno and Rome. Seen from thence, *Augusta Perusia* hangs like a storm cloud over her cliffs, impregnable but by strategy, as wicked and beautiful as ever her former masters, the Seven Deadly Sins, grandsons of Fortebraccio. The place is like its history, of course, having, in fact, grown up with it : you might say it was the incarnation of Perugia's spirit ; it would only be to admit, what is so obvious over here, that a town is the work of art of that larger soul, the body politic. So to see the crazy streets cut in steps and crevasses across and through the rocks, spanning a gorge with a stone ladder or boring a twisted tunnel under the sheer of the Etruscan walls, to note the churches innumerable and the foundations of the thirty fortress-towers she once had—all this is to read the secret of Perugia's two love affairs. Of her towers Julius II. left but two standing, blind pillars of masonry; but there were thirty of them once, and the Baglioni held them all, for a season. Now it was these wild Baglioni—"filling the town with all manner of evil living," says Matarazzo, but nevertheless intensely beloved for their bold bearing and beauty, as of young hawks;—it was just these blood-stained striplings, this Semonetto who rode shouting into the Piazza after an affray and swept his clogged hair clear of his eyes that he might see to kill, this black Astorre, "of the few words," who was murdered in his shirt on his marriage-eve by his cousin and best friend; it was this very cousin Grifone, so beautiful that "he seemed an angel of Paradise," who, in his turn, was cut down and laid out with his dead allies below San Lorenzo that his widow might not fail of finding him and his marred fairness—it was just this stormy crew that fell weeping at Suor Brigida's meek feet, confessed their sins, and received the Communion (encompassers and encompassed together, and all in a rapture) on the very eve of the great slaughter of 1500; it was they who adorned the Oratory of San Bernardino and made it the miracle of rose-colour and blue that it is; who reared the enormous San Domenico below the Gate of Mars, and who, in this hot-bed of enormity, nurtured Perugino's dreamy Madonnas. What it meant I know not at all. There are other riddles as hard in Umbria. Renan saw the gentle cadence of the landscape—violet hills, the silver gauze of water, oliveyards all of a green mist ; read the *Fioretti* and the dolorous ecstasies of Perugino's Sebastian, and straightway adapted the high-flown parallel worked out in detail by Giotto. Umbria for him was the Galilee of Italy, and Francis son of Bernard an *avatar* of Christ. But Renan was apt to allow his emotions to ride him.

Another dazzling contrast, which has re-
cently exercised another dextrous French-
man, is Siena with her Saint Catherine
and her Sodoma who betrayed her—Saint
Catherine, as great a force politically as
she was spiritually, and Sodoma, who
painted her like a Danaë with love-glazed
eyes fainting before the apparition of the
Crucified Seraph.

There is nothing like this in the history
of Tuscany, whose palaces not long were
fortresses nor her monks at any time suc-
cessful politicians. Cosimo had pulled
down the Florentine towers or ever the
last Oddi had loosed hold of Ridolfo's
throat. I know that Siena is just within
that province geographically ; in tempera-
ment, in art and manner, she has always
shown herself intensely Umbrian. Take,
then, the case of Savonarola. The Florentines received him gladly enough and heard
him with honest admiration, even enthusiasm. Still there is reason to believe they
took him, in the main, spectacularly, as
they also took that portentous old mono-
maniac Gemisthos Pletho, who made religions as we might make pills. For,
observe, Savonarola lost his head—and his

life, good soul !—where the Florentines did
not. The cobbler went beyond his last
when the *Frate* essayed politics. He suffered accordingly. But in Perugia, in Siena,
in Gubbio and Orvieto, the great revival-
ists Bernardine, Catherine, Fra Roberto,
held absolute rule over body and soul. For
the moment Baglione and Oddi kissed each
other ; all feuds were stayed ; a man
might climb the back alleys of a night without any fear of a knife to yerk him (the
Ancient's word) under the ribs or noose
round his neck to swing him up to the
archway withal. So Catherine brought
back Boniface (and much trouble) from
Avignon, and Da Lecce wrote out a new
constitution for some rock-bound hive of the
hills, whose crowd wailing in the market-
place knew the ecstasy of repentance, and
ran riot in religious orgies very much after
the fashion of the Greater Dionysia or, say, the
Salvation Army. And how Niccolò Alunno
would have painted the Salvation Army !

So it does seem that the two great
passions of Umbria burnt themselves out
together. They were, indeed, the two
ends of the candle. When the Baglioni
fell in the black work of two August nights,

only one escaped. And with them died
the love of the old lawless life and the infinite relish there was for some positive
foretaste of the life of the world to come.
Both lives had been lived too fast : from
that day Perugia fell into a torpor, as Perugino, the glass of his time and place, also
fell. Perugino, we know, had his doubts
concerning the immortality of the soul, but
painted on his beautiful cloister-dreams,
and knocked down his saints to the highest
bidder.* Vasari assures me that the chief
solace of the old prodigal in his end of days
was to dress his young wife's hair in fantastic coils and braids. A prodigal he was
—true Peruginese in that—prodigal of the
delicate meats his soul afforded. His end
may have been unedifying; it must at least
have been very pitiful. Nowadays his
name stands upon the Corso Vannucci of
the town he uttered, and in the court wall
of a little recessed and colonnaded house in
the Via Deliziosa. Meantime his frescos
drop mildewed from chapel walls or are
borne away to a pauper funeral in the
Palazzo Communale.

* See, however, what he has to say for himself in
Chapter V. *ante.*

In his finely studied *Sensations* M. Paul
Bourget, it seems to me, flogs the air and
fails to climb it when he struggles to lay
open the causes of poor Vannucci's embit-
tering. If ever painting took up the office
of literature it was in the fifteenth century.
The *quattrocentisti* stand to Italy for our
Elizabethan dramatists. This may have
produced bad painting: Mr. George Moore
will tell you that it did. I am not sure that
it very greatly matters, for, failing a literature which was really dramatic, really poet-
ical, really in any sense representative, it
was as well that there led an outlet somewhere. At any rate Lippi and Botticelli, to
those who know them, are expressive of
the Florentine temper when Pulci and Politian are distorted echoes of another; Perugino leads us into the recesses of Perugia
while Graziani keeps up fumbling at the
lock. And Perugino's languorous boys and
maids are the figments of a riotous erotic,
of a sensuous fancy without imagination or
intelligence or humour. His Alcibiades, or
Michael Archangel, seems greensick with a
love mainly physical; his Socrates has the
combed resignation of his Jeromes and
Romualds—smoothly ordered old men set

in the milky light of Umbrian mornings and dreaming out placid lives by the side of a moonfaced Umbrian beauty, who is now Mary and now Luna as chance motions his hand. How penetrating, how distinctive by the side of them seems Sandro's slim and tearful Anima Mundi shivering in the chill dawn ! With what a strange magic does Filippino usher in the pale apparition of the Mater Dolorosa to his Bernard, or flush her up again to a heaven of blue-green and a glory of burning cherubim ? This he does, you remember, with rocket-like effect in a chapel of the Minerva in Rome. But it is the unquenchable thirst of the Umbrians for some spiritual nutriment, some outlet for their passion to be found only in blood-shed or fainting below the Cross, some fierce and untamable animal quality such as you see to-day in the torn gables, the towers and bastions of Perugia, it is the spirit which informed and made these things you get in Perugino's pictures—in the hot sensualism of their colour-scheme, the ripe-ness and bloom of physical beauty encasing the vague longing of a too-rapid ado-lescence. The desire could never be fed and the bloom wore off. Look at Duccio's work on the façade of San Bernardino. Duccio was a Florentine, but where in Florence would you see his like ? What a revel of disproportion in these long - leg-ged nymphs, full-lipped and narrow-eyed as any of Rossetti's curious imagin-ings. Take the Povertà, a weedy girl with the shrinking paps of a child. Here again (exquisite as she is in modelling and intensity of ex-pression) you get the entice-ment of a mal-formation which is absolutely un-Greek—unless

you are to count Phrygia within the magic ring-fence—and only to be equalled by the luxury of Beccadelli. You get that in

Sodoma too, the handy Lombard; you have
it in Perugino and all the Umbrians (in some
form or other); but never, I think, in the
genuine Tuscan—not even in Botticelli—
and never, of course, in the Venetians.
Duccio modelled these things while the
Della Robbia were at their Hellenics; and a
few years after he did them, came the end
of the Baglioni and all such gear. The end
of real Umbrian art was not long. Perugino
awoke to have his doubts of the soul's immortality. No great wonder there, perhaps, given he acknowledged a merciful
heaven. . . .

I chanced to meet an old woman the
other day in a country omnibus. We journeyed together from Prato to Florence and
became very friendly. Your dry old woman, who hath had losses, who has become,
in fact, world-worn and very wise, or like
one of Shakespeare's veterans—the Grave-
digger, or the Countryman in *Antony and
Cleopatra*—has probed the ball and found it
hollow; such a battered and fortified soul
in petticoats is peculiar to Italy, and coun-
tries where the women work and the men,
pocketing their hands, keep sleek looks. We
had just passed a pleasant little procession.

It was Sunday, the hour Benediction. A staid nun was convoying a party of schoolgirls to church; whereupon I remarked to my neighbour on their pretty bearing, a sort of artless piety and of attention for unknown but not impossible blessings which they had about them. But my old woman took small comfort from it. She knew those cattle, she said: Capuchins, Jacobins, Black, White and Grey,—knew them all. Well! Everybody had his way of making a living: hers was knitting stockings. A hard life, *via*, but an honest. Here it became me to urge that the religious life might have its compensations, without which it would perhaps be harder than knitting stockings; that one needed relaxation and would do well to be sure that it was at least innocent. Relaxation of a kind, said she, a man must have. Snuff now! She was inveterate at the sport. The view was very dry; but I think it reasoned limitations also very Tuscan, and by no means exclusive of a tolerable amount of piety and honest dealing. Foligno, by mere contrast, reminds me of it—busy Foligno huddled between the mighty knees of a chalk down, city of falling churches and handsome girls, just now parading the streets with their fans a-flutter and a pretty turn to each veiled head of them.

As I write the light dies down, the wind drops, huge inky clouds hang over the west; the sun, as he falls behind them, sets them kindling at the edge. The worn old bleached domes, the bell-towers and turrets looming in the blue dusk, seem to sigh that the century moves so slowly forward. How many more must they endure of these? It is the hour of *Ave Maria*. But only two cracked bells ring it in.

LOVELY and honourable ladies, it is, as I hold, no mean favour you have accorded me, to sit still and smiling while I have sung to your very faces a stave verging here and there on the familiar. You have sat thus enduring me, because, being wrought for the most part out of stone or painter's stuff, your necessities have indeed forbidden retirement. Yet my obligations should not on that account be lighter. He would be a thin spirit who should gain a lady's friendly regard, and then vilipend because she knew no better, or could not choose. I hope indeed that I have done you no wrong, *gentildonne*. I protest that I have meant none ; but have loved you all as a man may, who has, at most, but a bowing acquaintance with your ladyships. As I recall your starry names, no blush hinting unmannerliness suspect and unconfessed hits me on the cheek :—Simonetta, Ilaria, Nenciozza, Bettina ; you too, candid Mariota of Prato ; you, flinching little

Imola; and you, snuff-taking, wool-carding
ancient lady of the omnibus—scorner of
monks, I have kissed your hands. I have
at least given our whole commerce frankly
to the world ; and I know not how any
shall say we have been closer acquainted
than we should. You, tall Ligurian Simonetta, loved of Sandro, mourned by Giuliano
and, for a season, by his twisted brother
and lord, have I done well to utter but one
side of your wild humour ? The side a
man would take, struck, as your Sandro
was, by a nympholepsy, or, as Lorenzo
was, by the rhymer's appetite for where-
withal to sonnetteer ? If I understand you,
it was never pique or a young girl's petu-
lance drove you to Phrynè's one justifiable
act of self-assertion. It was honesty,
Madonna, or I have read your grey eyes in
vain ; it was enthusiasm—that flame of our
fire so sacred that though it play the incen-
diary there shall be no crime—or where
would be now the "Vas d'elezione"?—
nor though it reveal a bystander's grin,
any shame at all. I shall live to tell that
story of thine, Lady Simonetta, to thy
honour and my own respect; for, as a poet
says,

" There is no holier flame
Than flutters torchwise in a stripling heart,
.   .   .   .   .   a fire from Heaven
To ash the clay of us, and wing the God."

I have seen all memorials of you left
behind to be pondered by him who played
Dante to your Beatrice, Sandro the painting
poet,—the proud clearness of you as at the
marriage feast of Nastagio degli Onesti; the
melting of the sorrow that wells from you
in a tide, where you hold the book of your
over-mastering honour and read *Magnificat
Anima Mea* with a sob in your throat ; your
acquaintance, too, with that grief which
was your own hardening ; your sojourn,
wan and woebegone as would become the
wife of Moses (maker of jealous gods) ;
all these guises of you, as well as the
presentments of your innocent youth, I
have seen and adored.   But I have ever
loved you most where you stand a wistful
Venus Anadyomenè—"Una donzella non
con uman volto," as Politian confessed ; for
I know your heart, Madonna, and see on
the sharp edge of your threatened life,
Ardour look back to maiden Reclusion, and
on (with a pang of foreboding) to mockery
and evil judgment.   Never fear but I brave

your story out to the world ere many days. And if any, with profane leer and tongue in the cheek, take your sorrow for reproach or your pitifulness for a shame, let them receive the lash of the whip from one who will trouble to wield it : *non ragioniam di lor.* For your honourable women I give you Ilaria, the slim Lucchesan, and my little Bettincina, a child yet with none of the vaguer surmises of adolescence when it flushes and dawns, but likely enough, if all prosper, to be no shame to your company. As yet she is aptest to Donatello's fancy: she will grow to be of a statelier bevy. I see her in Ghirlandajo's garden, pacing, still-eyed, calm and cold, with Ginevra de' Benci and Giovanna of the Albizzi, those quiet streets on a visit to the mother of John Baptist.

Mariota, the hardy wife of the metal-smith, is not for one of your quality, though the wench is well enough now with her baby on her arm and the best of her seen by a poet and made enduring. He, like our Bernardo, had motherhood in such esteem that he held it would ransom a sin. A sin? I am no casuist to discuss rewards and punishments ; but if Socrates were rightly informed and sin indeed ignorance, I have no whips for Mariota's square shoulders. Her baby, I warrant, plucked her from the burning. I am not so sure but you might find in that girl a responsive spirit, and—is the saying too hard?—a teacher. Contentment with a few things was never one of your virtues, madam.

There is a lady whose name has been whispered through my pages, a lady with whom I must make peace if I can. Had I known her, as Dante did, in the time of her nine-year excellence and followed her (with an interlude, to be sure, for Gentucca) through the slippery ways of two lives with much eating of salt bread, I might have grown into her favour. But I never did know Monna Beatrice Portinari; and when I met her afterwards as my Lady Theologia I thought her something imperious and case-hardened. Now here and there some words of mine (for she has a high stomach) may have given offence. I have hinted that her court is a slender one in Italy, the service paid her lip-service; the lowered eyes and bated breath reserved for her; but for Fede her sister, tears and long kisses

and the clinging. Well! the Casa Catto-
licà is a broad foundation; I find Francis of
Umbria at the same board with Sicilian
Thomas. If I cleave to the one must I
despise the other? Lady Fede has my
heart and Lady Dottrina must put aside the
birch if she would share that little kingdom.
Religio habet, said Pico; *theologia autem
invenit.* Let her find. But she must be
speedy, for I promise her the mood grows
on me as I become *italianato ;* and I cannot predict when the other term of the
proposition may be accomplished. For
one thing, Lady Theologia, I praise you
not. Sympathy seems to me of the essence, the healing touch an excellent thing
in woman. But you told Virgil,

> " Io son fatta da Dio, sua mercè, tale,
> Che la vostra miseria non mi tange."

Sympathy, Madonna? And Virgil hope-
less! On these terms I had rather gloom
with the good poet (whose fault in your
eyes was that he knew in what he had
believed) than freeze with you and Aquinas
on your peak of hyaline. And as I have
found you, Donna Beatrice, so in the main
have they of whom I pitch my pipe. Here

and there a man of them got exercise for his fingers in your web; here and there one, as Pico the young Doctor of yellow hair and nine hundred heresies, touched upon the back of your ivory dais that he might jump from thence to the poets out beyond you in the Sun. Your great Dante, too, loved you through all. But, Madonna, he had loved you before when you were—

Donna pietosa e di novella etade,

and, as became his lordly soul, might never depart from the faith he had in you. For me, I protest I love Religion your warm-bosomed mate too well to turn from her; yet I would not on that account grieve her (who treats you well out of the cup of her abounding charity) by aspersing you. And if I may not kiss your foot as you would desire, I may bow when I am in the way with you; not thanking God I am not as you are, but, withal, wishing you that degree of interest in a really excellent world with which He has blessed me and my like, the humble fry.

Lastly, to the Spirits which are in the shrines of the cities of Tuscany, I lift up my hands with the offering of my thin

book. To Lucca dove-like and demure, to
Prato, the brown country-girl, to Pisa,
winsome maid-of-honour to the lady of
the land, to Pistoja, the ruddy-haired and
ample, and to Siena, the lovely wretch,
black-eyed and keen as a hawk; even to
Perugia, the termagant, with a scar on her
throat; but chiefest to the Lady Firenze,
the pale Queen crowned with olive—to all
of you, adored and adorable sisters, I offer
homage as becomes a postulant, the repentance of him who has not earned his
reward, thanksgiving, and the praise I have
not been able to utter. And I send you,
Book, out to those ladies with the suppli-
cation of good Master Cino, schoolman and
poet, saying,

> E se tu troverai donne gentile,
> Ivi girai ; chè là ti vo mandare ;
> E dono a lor d' audienza chiedi.
>
> Poi di a costor: Gittatevi a lor piedi,
> E dite, chi vi manda e per che fare,
> Udite donne, esti valletti umili.

www.ingramcontent.com/pod-product-compliance
Lightning Source LLC
Chambersburg PA
CBHW020600260626
47157CB00003B/797